The
Prodigal

Anthem To The Wind/Book 2

Don Horne

HORNE PUBLISHING

RED OAK, TEXAS

The Prodigal

Anthem To The Wind
/Book 2

To order, or for quantities:

ISBN 13 – 978-0615459639

ISBN 10 - 0615459633

www.amazon.com

And Other Book Retailers

**Horne Publishing
302 Cascade Drive
Red Oak, Texas 75154**

This story and events are a work of fiction. The story takes place in a historical context, but the names in the story are only coincidentally similar to people either living or dead.

Dedication

Our American legacy is based on the true stories of sacrifice, hard work, and family interaction such as this story. Stories my grand-mother told me are so much more interesting and thought provoking than the ones I could make up. I was, and still am, proud of my immigrant forefathers that came and built a country out of the wilderness called America. Never asking for, or taking, a handout, all they ever asked was an opportunity to become an American.

Acknowledgments

Very little one accomplishes in life, business, education, or building a play house, is done alone. This is the second in a two part book that could never have taken place without the help of others.

I wish to thank and acknowledge the help of my friends and family. All are teachers and with their editing and support, I am sure this is a better product. My wife especially had to read and reread and convince me what I had written could be improved. So, a special thanks to her.

Preface

Berlin, Germany, 1945

Hans Gruber, former Nazi SS assassin, and now working for the Soviets in the aftermath of World War II, had been shadowing the young American Army officer for over two hours. Hans had been alerted by a double agent on the inside of the occupying allied military about a secret document transfer, and was sitting in his car waiting for a courier to come out of the Army headquarters building. Finally, a tall, fit looking, American Army officer emerged with a briefcase handcuffed to his left wrist. He looked side to side and got in a jeep parked at the curb.

Although he made sure he tailed him at a distance in his black 1934 Mercedes sedan, Hans followed him all over the city as the American ran a circuitous course to "shake" or lose someone if he was being followed. Finally, the man seemed to have convinced himself he was alone.

Hans sat in his car and watched the American park his jeep in front of the White Lily Pub and Bar, which was in a partially bombed out building, one of only a few with very little damage, not far from downtown Berlin. The young officer looked at his watch, disembarked, and started walking slowly among the burnt out buildings as if he were sightseeing. He looked up and down shaking his head at the destruction, obviously in no hurry for his appointment.

"How trusting these young Americans are!" Hans thought to himself. He was confident this was going to be easy. He did not follow the young man, but was content to wait and let him come to him. He sat down outside the pub on the patio at a small table for two, and ordered a dark German beer as he watched him with his peripheral vision. The American, after a few minutes, took another look at his watch and turned around to head back to the pub. Hans knew he needed to make his move before the officer met his appointment and gave away the briefcase.

Hans watched the entrance to the restroom.

He knew most Americans wash their hands before they eat. The American looked around to satisfy himself his party had not arrived, and walked directly to the restroom which was off the floor of the restaurant, down a small hall lit with only one bare electric light. The door opened outward, and once inside, the room had seen better days. It smelled of urine and filth from not having a regular cleaning. It was dim lit and Hans waited a moment to allow his eyes to adjust. At the other end of a row of urinals the young American was standing looking down. Hans had looked and made sure the hallway was empty before entering. He shut the door behind him and started to reach for his Luger in a hidden shoulder holster under his suit coat.

"I've been waiting for you to make your move, Gerry. I have known since headquarters you were following me."

The slight drawl, thought Hans to himself, placed the American as being from somewhere in the South in the United States. His hand froze on his pistol as he looked and realized the man had turned toward him. Hans was facing an Army issue Colt 45 in the hand of a steely-eyed young Army officer that showed no sign of fear or wavering.

"The war is over, you know. You lost."

"Not for me it isn't!" Hans' hand jerked on the butt of the Luger, and as it cleared the holster the American shot him twice through the heart. He staggered back against the stucco wall as his pistol fell clattering on the tile floor.

His hand went to his chest and came away dripping blood, and he slid down the wall to a sitting position leaving a trail of crimson. As his eyes began to dim in death, Hans could only cringe slightly as the man leaned over him and spoke to him quietly.

"That's where you're wrong, Gerry. It's over especially for you!" was all he said.

Captain Austin Johnson of the 6th United States Army T-Force hurriedly searched the man: found several passports, sets of papers, and a fat wallet with three thousand American dollars in hundred dollar bills. He took one passport for Switzerland and one for England. He also took out all but three one hundred dollar bills.

The door burst open and two Army

sergeant MP's, were pointing their own 45's at him as they stood in the doorway.

"Man, I am so glad you are here! He drew a gun and made a grab for my briefcase. I had noticed him following me and so I came in here. I already had my pistol in my hand pretending to be going to the toilet when he came through the door. As he reached in his shoulder holster, I shot him."

The two men looked at one another and lowered their pistols. One of the men happened to recognize Austin as being from head-quarters.

"Good job, Captain!"

"Listen, men, he obviously is a spy or assassin of some sort. I searched him and in his wallet he had a snapshot of him and a girl in

11

front of a Nazi flag. One of the passports he was carrying is German and has his name as Hans Gruber. I am here to meet up with a British diplomat and deliver some important documents. Can you men take over from here?"

The men nodded.

Austin smiled, "I will be glad to say in my report the wallet was empty."

The two men looked at one another. They were used to finding people shot and having few facts to back up what happened. After the three hundred dollar gift, they were willing to swear they found Gruber dead already when they burst into the restroom, and they were not going to even mention the Army officer.

"Thanks men, I will see you on the base. I'll

buy the first round!"

"Sure! Sure! You got a deal, captain! Get outta here!"

They both patted him on the back as he went by them out the door, down the hallway and out the back. By that time people were coming into the pub to see what had happened. He jogged around to his jeep to find a stunning blonde in a British officer's uniform sitting in the front passenger's seat holding a large manila envelope and a small clutch purse. She smiled at him and said, "Captain Johnson, my name is Hannah Olsen, and I believe we need to have a sense of urgency about leaving this area!"

Austin grinned at the woman's use of the King's English as he vaulted over the door opening, turned on the ignition switch, hit the floor starter in the jeep, and without spinning the tires, accelerated hard enough to push them both into their seats as they fled down the street and turned the first corner which came up after a few blocks.

Once they were a few more blocks away from the pub, Austin slowed the jeep to just fast enough to have a conversation and still not draw any undue attention.

The woman said. "You can give me the briefcase now and I will take over from here."

Austin looked quickly at her and said, "I had instructions to meet a Dr. Barnhardt here and escort him to the British sector."

She smiled at him and said, "Don't you trust me?"

He had slowed the jeep to just more than a crawl to go around piles of bricks and lumber lying in the street. It was the shattered carcass of the once proud Third Reich.

He looked into her gorgeous green eyes and said flatly, "No."

Flustered momentarily, she asked, "Why not?"

"No offense, but actually I have not seen anything to make me trust you. A man I never saw before somehow knew I was coming, and tried to kill me in the restroom. I get to my jeep and the most beautiful woman I have ever seen in my life is sitting there. How did you know that was my jeep?"

"By the time I arrived, the jeep was the only military vehicle I saw."

"Where is <u>your</u> vehicle?"

"I was dropped off because I was told you would take me to where I wanted to go."

"Then how were you going to *take over from here*, to use your choice of words?"

Although her left hand still held the envelope, her right hand was in her lap as if to inch inside her small purse.

"Furthermore, Hannah Olsen, or whatever your name is, if you start to pull anything except a compact out of that purse, I am going to punch your lights out!"

She was startled for a moment by his sharp tone and quick transformation from a hillbilly soldier to a deadly foe. She looked at him for a moment, and quietly said, "I think you would, Captain Johnson. I think you would."

16

"And another thing, how do you know my name?"

"Find a lit place where we can have some privacy, and I will show you my identification as a British officer. I am Royal Secret Service similar to you and my code name is Dr. Barnhardt. I was sent to meet you."

For the first time, Austin relaxed a little and even smiled, "Fair enough."

He thought to himself, "Killing Gruber was one thing, but I would hate to have to hurt a woman as beautiful as this one!"

Austin stopped the jeep under one of the very few working street lamps and checked her identification. He still held on to the briefcase, however. He would wait until they got to the British sector checkpoint and he could give the briefcase over to her with witnesses. Whatever was in the briefcase was important enough to have already cost one life, and he did not want the next one to be his.

Chapter One

Little Rock, Arkansas 1940

Austin and James Johnson, and their first cousin, Anna Johnson, had just finished playing tennis at the Little Rock Country club and were sitting watching the others play from under an umbrella furnished with a table and chairs. There were several courts at play with mostly young adults.

"Wow, Anna, you were awesome today! Why you almost won several games from Jimmy and me!" When Austin laughed, Anna frowned, ran her hand through her short, blonde hair, and replied back.

"If I had had a woman for a partner instead of a clumsy man I would have beaten you bad!"

"Come on, Jerry Allen is a pretty good tennis player. You are just sore because we won."

"I don't suppose you want to take me on in singles, do you?"

"I don't think so. You think you could probably take me, and truthfully, you might!"

Anna smiled then at Austin's attempt to make peace. On her best day and Austin on his worst, she knew he would beat her. Austin was a great athlete just like his dad, Luke Johnson.

It was a hot June day in 1940. The heat rose off the painted asphalt tennis court in shimmering waves. Although all were already tan, the heat made the sweat soak their clothes and drip from foreheads and legs. They were discussing where to go and when to get out of the stifling heat.

Austin and Anna were close enough in age to have been in the same high school class. Both had just graduated with honors and Anna was the Valedictorian. Austin was Salutatorian. Both were on their way to the University of Arkansas in the fall, and Austin was to leave in a few weeks to start football practices. He had been a state champion quarterback at Little Rock High School. Anna had already tried out and won a position as a cheerleader and would go to The University at the same time.

James, his younger brother, was the heir

apparent to the quarterback position for the Little Rock High School, and had played backup to Austin for the last two years. All three were very close friends.

"Let's go get a Coke and a hamburger somewhere!" exclaimed Anna. "I want to drive your new car."

"Now, wait a minute. My mother doesn't even drive my car."

"Well, I am not your mother!" She giggled a victorious laugh as Austin handed her the keys.

Austin and James looked at one another and just shook their heads as if there were no use in arguing. The truth is, Anna, Austin, and James, when he was old enough, all had a drivers license. In Arkansas the legal age to drive a car was 14. The legal age to fly an airplane was 16, and all three had their pilot's licenses also. Luke and Levi, their dads, had been pilots and instructors since World War I.

All had flown solo, and could fly well long before they were of legal age. Anna had met Amelia Earhart in 1936, and was devastated after her apparent death the next year. She had vowed to continue her legacy. Anna had her blonde hair cut short just like Amelia. She still had a picture Amelia had signed of her and Anna at an air show in 1936. She wore riding pants more often than dresses unless she was going out. Kathryn Hepburn, the pants-dressing movie star, was her new idol.

She was "worshiped from afar" by most of the young men at school and the country club for she could be merciless with her sharp wit and in her criticisms of the young men. Still, Anna had more friends that were male than female for she had no time for giggling, frilly dressed girls her own age.

The threesome inserted their wooden tennis racquets in their presses to keep them from warping, picked up their towels and balls, and started toward the shiny, new, black 1940 Ford Deluxe convertible which was Austin's graduation present from his parents for a job well done.

James had jumped up and down with excitement to inherit his mother's red 1936 Ford convertible, which Austin had been driving before. James was the one which had kept it washed and waxed, and while Austin drove their dad's Cadillac on his dates, James was perfectly satisfied to drive the little red Ford roadster. Austin receiving a car for graduation had made James a happy man.

Anna and Austin opened the doors and undid the convertible latches on the inside just above the windshield header, and all three helped fold and stow the top. Just as they finished, a duet of very pretty twin girls dressed in tennis outfits from James' high school class walked up to the car. They were twins although one was blonde and one was brunette. The especially pretty brunette named Payton spoke up in a melodious voice, "Hi Jimmy. Can Mallory and I go with you?"

James looked at Austin and Anna, smiled, and said, "Sure, why not? I had rather drive my own car anyway."

Both girls squeezed into the seat with Payton next to James, who was grinning ear to ear. Austin and Anna laughed to see the threesome and knew he was in good hands.

James turned on the key, pushed the dash mounted starter button, and smiled as the engine started almost as quickly as an electric motor. The car barely had 10,000 miles and was in perfect shape.

The 1936 Ford had a three speed shifter in the floor, and as he put the transmission into first gear he touched Payton's bare knee. His face reddened as he said quickly, "I am so sorry!"

Both girls laughed and Payton said, "Aw come on, Jimmy. Girls aren't stupid. You did that on purpose!"

As James' face got even more red, and he was getting tongue-tied trying to apologize, the girls were laughing hard at him. He finally laughed too when he realized the tease.

Once at the drive-in, both boys pulled their cars in under the shade of the overhang and at once were surrounded by laughing and loud youths. The Johnson boys and Anna were very popular.

"Nice car!" exclaimed the carhop as she skated up to the driver's side. Jill was a year out of high school and knew the threesome very well as she did all of the regulars. She had on a red short skating skirt and a white knit shirt with striping on the sleeves and collar. There was a patch which read, "Red's Drive-

In."

Reluctant to have to admit it wasn't hers, Anna said, "It actually belongs to Austin and I had to beat him in tennis to get to drive it."

"Yeah, right. I don't believe that. Now, what can I get for you guys?"

"Two hamburgers and two orders of fries. I want a cherry coke and he will have a chocolate shake."

The girl looked at Austin, and in a very flirtatious voice said, "Don't you talk?"

"I only get to talk when she stops to take a breath."

Austin and the carhop laughed as Anna frowned and hit him on the arm. The girl smirked at Anna who stuck out her tongue at her as the girl skated away laughing.

"You are so mean to me, Austin Johnson!"

"I am just trying to keep you humble."

A handsome young man in a white knit shirt and pressed Bermuda shorts separated himself from a group of guys and started walking toward the car.

"Here comes Mr. Cool," grinned Austin.

"Oh great," said Anna, but her smile gave her away. Of all the rich, handsome men in school, Ben Winston was one of the few she would talk to. He amused her because he was so full of himself, and she made fun of him just to belittle him.

"Hi, Benny. I didn't see you on the tennis court this morning."

"Nah, I got up late. I just came by to pick up lunch."

Austin smiled to himself. Benjamin Winston the Third did not like to get sweaty or dirty. He looked like he had just stepped out of the bath and into freshly pressed shorts. No one wore pressed tennis shorts but Benny. His nose in the air posture and arched eyebrows irritated Austin. Just once he would like to throw him into a mudhole. The thought left a smile on his face as he nodded to him.

"Call me when the burgers come. I am going to go check on James."

Austin got out of the car, and before he could walk the few feet to James and the girls, he had a girl on either arm. He looked back at Anna and winked. She was smiling and just shaking her head. She was proud to know Austin and James were related to her.

Austin invited all the kids at the drive-in to his house to go swimming at 6 p.m. He called home and his mother gave her permission. She told him to stop by the Tanner's Market on the way home and she would call in and place an order for the items for the party.

Everyone was excited for the Johnsons lived on 20 acres of manicured landscaping with a swimming pool, tennis court, basketball court, and enough room with a backstop to play softball. On top of that, they had a middle-aged Chinese man and wife, John and Lydia Wong, to cook and serve.

The big, walled estate was on Cantrell Road overlooking the Arkansas River. The house itself sat well back from the road with a circular drive up front and a six car garage behind the house. The front drive had a covering in front of the house in case of inclement weather for visitors to disembark.

The huge double doors opened into a tiled foyer with a double staircase to the second floor. The ceiling in the foyer was two stories tall. There was a large library on the ground floor as well as a smaller one on the second. The master bedroom was on the second floor as well as an office for Luke to do his business. The small library was next to the bedroom. The house had six bedrooms, the pool house had a party room with separate showers and restrooms.

By 6:30 p.m. the place was full of loud, laughing young people. John Wong and his wife Lydia were hard pressed to keep up with hamburgers and hot dogs for everyone. John and Lydia were Chinese and had been part of the Johnson household for over 15 years. The Johnsons; Luke, Maddie, Austin, and James, treated them like family.

Austin saw what was happening, and put on a chef hat and apron over his swim trunks. He took the spatula out of the hand of a protesting John Wong's hand and said, "You serve this crowd, and I will cook!"

"Thank you, Master Austin. This very big group. Are you sure you know all these people?" His slight accent was showing.

Austin laughed, "Probably not, but it doesn't matter. Mom bought enough food for half of Little Rock!"

Luke and Maddie Johnson, Austin and

James' parents, came out of the house with a large push cart full of ice and two wooden, hand cranked, ice cream mixers. A shout went up from the kids and a line formed to crank the handles. Salt was poured over the ice and the handles were being cranked so hard the kids had to be told to slow it down some to let the ice cream harden. Finally, the crank became harder and harder to turn and Luke stopped the young man on the first handle, opened up the container and announced, "It's ready!"

There were shouts and squeals of delight as the ice cream was put into bowls and Maddie and Lydia had cut up bananas and strawberries for toppings to go with the chocolate and caramel syrup flavorings. Lydia scraped out the containers, went inside and rinsed them out, and refilled them with more ice cream mix. This time she added a bottle of Orange Crush to give the ice cream an orange color and taste. Again, the kids were pressing forward with their bowls and after two more creamers full everyone decided they had had enough.

Even after being warned by Maddie to not go in swimming for at least 30 minutes after eating, there were several which jumped into the pool, splashing everyone. Over half of the huge pool was only chest deep and people were enjoying standing and splashing one another. Maddie smiled and shook her head. She knew from her own experience it was hopeless to remind youngsters to wait. She didn't, and the kids didn't.

The younger kids started leaving by 9 p.m. and by 10 just the older kids were left sitting by the pool or sitting on the edge and dangling their feet in the water. The conversations ranged from celebrities to sports, and there were lots of concerns about going off to college in the fall when the world looked so unsettled. Germany had already invaded Poland and everyone questioned how long before they dragged the rest of the world into a war.

Austin and Mallory, and James and Payton, were on one side of the pool while Anna was on the other side sitting between Jerry Allen and Benny Winston. Anna got up just as two muscular football player friends of Austin and James approached her.

"Anna!" said Fred, who was the biggest.

"Whut?" answered Anna in a voice full of sarcasm, making everyone laugh.

Somewhat embarrassed, Fred continued. "Mike and I think you need to take a swim."

"It took <u>two</u> of you to arrive at that decision? Does that mean you each have only half a brain? I am on my way to get a Coke. I don't want to get wet again, and, besides, I don't have time to play games with children!"

The group was suddenly quiet for the two boys were several inches taller and several pounds heavier than Anna's five foot five frame.

"Is it going to be a problem with you and James if we throw her in the pool?" asked Fred, looking directly at Austin. He did not want to have to confront Austin and James.

"Listen, Fred, <u>you</u> are the one with the problem if you try to throw her in the pool. She can more than take care of herself, but don't say I didn't warn you."

Austin and James smiled at one another as the two approached Anna. Fred put his hand out as if to grab her, but Anna grabbed his wrist, twisted her body under him and threw him over her shoulder into the pool.

Mike also made a grab but was grasping at air as she neatly sidestepped him, pulled his out stretched arm toward her, and with his own momentum yanked him sideways and let him go. He was flailing his arms as he yelled out, and he too went backwards into the pool.

"Now, leave me alone!"

Everyone stared in silent unbelief at the two

hapless young men sputtering in the pool. Anna walked the few steps over to the edge of the patio, dipped her hand into the wash tub filled with ice and cold drinks, and picked out a bottle of Coca Cola. She pried open the bottle with the opener attached to the tub handle with a string, took a long drink, and looked back at the crowd of kids who were still staring silently with their mouths open.

"Now what? Haven't you ever seen anybody drink a Coke before?"

Austin and James laughed at what had happened, and went to the edge of the pool and offered their friends assistance in getting out of the pool. Fred and Mike were standing on the edge of the pool dripping.

"What happened?" asked Fred. "Where did

she learn that stuff?"

"Our main man, John Wong, is a Chinese martial arts expert, and we have all been taking lessons since we could walk. I tried to warn you."

Fred knew he had been had and he smiled at Austin and said, "You could have tried a little bit harder to warn me. She's dangerous!"

Both laughed, and Fred put his head closer to Austin and said just above a whisper, "Do you think she would go out with me?"

Austin's surprise was showing on his face as he said, "Now let me understand this. She just threw you in the pool, and you want to ask her out?"

"Yeah," Fred muttered sheepishly, as he shook his head up and down.

"Tell you what. You ask her out after you apologize, and if she doesn't throw you in the pool again you have your answer!"

Austin patted him on the shoulder as he handed him a dry towel with a smile and said, "Good luck!"

As the group of kids from the party left, Fred hung around Austin and James and finally saw Anna alone. She was helping pick up towels and leftovers from the party. He walked over by her, picked up a pair of towels, handed them to her, and said, "I apologize."

"Why?" smiled Anna. "I am not the one that was in the pool."

He looked down for a moment, and said, "The truth is, I wanted you to notice me."

"Well, I think <u>everyone</u> noticed you," she

41

laughed.

"Would you go out with me?" Fred blurted.

Anna studied him for a moment with her smile mostly gone as she questioned to herself if he was kidding or not. What Fred did not know is Anna had already decided back in grade school she liked him. She smiled a small, enigmatic smile, and said, "Yes, Fred Tanner, I would like that, but only if we don't go swimming."

"You don't have to worry about that!"

As she escorted him to his car, she put her arm through his. They made a date for the next night to go to the movies to see *Gone With The Wind*. He was to pick her up early enough to take her out to eat. At the car he put his arms around her and she smiled at him.

"I suppose I should apologize, Fred. I was a little hard on you."

"It's okay, really. Little things like I need to leave you alone and keep my hands to myself are things I need to know."

She giggled and kissed him quickly on the cheek and whispered, "See you tomorrow!"

Anna stood and waved as Fred drove away in his dad's red, 1940 Chevrolet convertible. His dad owned several large grocery stores in Little Rock and North Little Rock, and although he said it was his car, Fred drove it so much no one believed him.

Austin and James walked up beside Anna, and Austin teased, "Now I know how to pick up girls! I let them throw me in the pool."

Anna smiled. "I thought I was going to

have to grab him and throw him in myself. I am glad he thought of the idea. I wanted some way to break the ice with him."

All three laughed and James said, "I think you could safely say the ice is broken!"

The three best friends were laughing as they walked arm in arm into the house. Maddie watched through the kitchen window and smiled to herself. She remembered a time when she and Luke, and his twin brother, Levi, were just that close back home in Paris, Arkansas. It seemed so long ago at times, but reliving her childhood through the lives of her boys and Anna made it seem like just yesterday. She was still smiling as Luke put his arm around her to see what had made her smile.

"I remember those times too, Maddie Johnson. Anna is just as independent as if she were your own child. If I didn't know better, I would think you were training her!"

"Well, we do talk a lot about boys and stuff."

Luke shook his head and hugged Maddie to him and said, "I knew it! You have been responsible all along! You took that sweet little girl and turned her into another Maddie. Lord help us!"

They were both still smiling as the kids came into the kitchen through the patio doors. Seeing their parents smiling at them, both boys frowned as if they did not like to be the object of their affection. However, Anna smiled back.

"Is my room ready? I am tired," said Anna.

"You do know this is not where you live," smiled Maddie.

"Really? Then why do you have a bedroom just for me?"

"When you were little, you played so much and so long here at our house you would fall asleep, and it was easier to call your parents and put you to bed than to get in the car and take you the couple of miles to your house."

"Thank you, Aunt Maddie. I have already called home, and I needed to visit with you anyway. Fred Tanner asked me out after I threw him into the pool."

"Men are such weird, simple little creatures, aren't they? When we were kids I used to make Luke chase me, and I would only run just fast enough to let him catch me. He never caught on."

Luke put his arm around Maddie again and said, "That is why I was in such good shape for sports. It came from chasing her!"

They all had a good laugh and Maddie and Anna walked arm in arm up the stairs to go to her bedroom. Lydia Wong came into the room to ask if there was anything else they wanted of her and John, and after being told she and John had done a good job at the party, they smiled, bowed, and went out the door to their quarters in the back.

Later, as Maddie sat at her dressing table and brushed her hair, Luke asked what she and Anna had talked about.

"Oh, it was just girl stuff. Our little Anna has her first crush and her first real date. I am feeling really old at how much she has matured."

"Yeah, I can see what you mean. Like throwing boys into the swimming pool!"

Both laughed for they could remember similar times from their own youth.

"Truth is," smiled Austin. "I bet he knows now to keep his hands to himself!"

Maddie smiled at him in the mirror and said, "Thankfully, they <u>never</u> learn that lesson."

"What else did you two talk about?"

"She told me she and Fred were going with Jimmy and Payton to see *Gone With The Wind* tomorrow night. She was so excited to finally get to go out with him. He had been the only boy she had had a crush on since they were in grade school."

"Well, he must have liked her also to ask her out after she threw him and Mike into the pool."

Maddie and Luke smiled as they both remembered a time when she had hit him in the stomach in Paris in the well house when he had teased her. She had tried to get away and go back to the dance, but he grabbed her and held her off the ground while he kissed her.

"I guess I did not move fast enough that night."

"Maddie, you moved just fast enough for me to catch you! You wanted me to kiss you!"

"I confess. Try it again and this time I won't run," she said smiling at him.

"It still seems as if Anna should be the little

blonde 5 year old chasing the tennis balls on the court, or the 10 year old hitting the ball by the hour against the wall. She could beat anybody except Austin among her friends."

"Turn the light out, Uncle Luke, and come to bed."

Chapter Two

The next day was Friday, and Austin, up early as usual, was sitting out by the pool with a cup of black coffee. James and Anna usually slept to mid morning until the smell of coffee and breakfast cooked by John and Lydia woke them.

"Mind if I join you?"

"No, of course not, Dad."

"I am sorry, son. I have taught you a bad habit of getting up early. Your mother would sleep until she starved to death if someone did not wake her!"

They both laughed and Luke admitted, "Okay, maybe it is not that bad. All the sleep she gets is why she is still so beautiful."

It was no secret to anyone who knew the Johnsons how beautiful Maddie Johnson was compared to any other middle-aged woman they knew, including celebrities. Although she secretly colored her hair a little, even the young guys looked as she walked by in town or at the pool. Luke was still very fit as an ex-boxer and athlete. He worked out regularly at the fitness center in the country club with Austin and James, and he still could more than hold his own at tennis, handball, and golf. At 49 years of age he was not looking with glee at turning 50 on August the 5th.

"Hey, I hear James and Anna both have

dates tonight, what are you doing?"

"I guess I am taking Mallory Potter, Payton's twin sister, but she is such a kid."

"She is just a year younger than you, and she is gorgeous! I bet every guy in Little Rock would love to take her out."

Austin smiled and said, "Well, I am actually proud of taking her out and being seen with her. This will be our third date, and I think Mom is already planning a wedding!"

They both smiled and shook their heads for both Maddie and Luke thought Austin was old enough to have a girlfriend. The thought of a girlfriend to Austin was fine, but he wanted to still be able to see what the women were like at the University of Arkansas.

The movie, *Gone With The Wind*, was to

begin at six o'clock, and Fred came for Anna at four o'clock, who was still at her aunt and uncle's house. Austin and James were to pick up their dates at the same time, and all three couples were to meet at the Italian restaurant across the street from the new Palace movie theater in downtown Little Rock. They wanted to get there early to sit in the balcony where the ushers with their flashlights did not patrol so much. Couples with children sat on the downstairs or main floor. It was no secret, but it was an unspoken custom of most classy theaters. The couples also knew a line would start to form about 5 p.m., and they did not want to stand in line very long.

The three couples were almost first in line. As they stepped up to pay, the teen age girl selling tickets smiled at Austin and said, "That will be one dollar apiece."

Austin, who was buying for everyone, asked, "Why so much? On most Saturdays we can see a double feature and a cartoon for only twenty-five cents!"

"It is a special movie, and it is real long. It even has an intermission. I don't set the prices anyway."

Austin smiled at the girl to let her know he was kidding, and she smiled back and said, "You are an onery cuss, aren't you?"

Austin handed her a ten dollar bill for everyone's tickets. Anna, who knew the girl from school, said into the talk opening of the booth, "Yes, Janie, he is always like that. Don't pay any attention to him."

Janie put her head close to Anna and said in a low voice, "I wish he <u>would</u> pay attention to me!"

"I will put in a good word for you."

Both girls smiled at one another as the little group hurried up to the balcony. As soon as the lights went down for the movie to start, everyone took their dates' hands except Austin and Mallory. Anna squeezed Austin's arm, and when he turned to look at her, she looked down at her and Fred's hands and nodded toward Mallory. Austin rolled his eyes and put his hand over his date's hand. She turned and smiled at him, turned her hand over, and started holding his hand. Austin leaned over to Anna and whispered, "Would you quit trying to run my life?"

"You are so dense sometimes, Austin Johnson. Someone needs to teach you some etiquette and manners about going out on a date!" she whispered back.

She patted Austin's arm and smiled as she leaned over and put her head on Fred's shoulder who was smiling broadly and thinking to himself it was definitely worth a dip in the pool to be holding Anna Johnson's hand.

After the long movie, all three couples stopped for Cokes at the drive in, and as Austin and James took their dates home, Fred and Anna went to her house.

Levi and Ellen Johnson's home was similar in size and design to Luke and Maddie's, for Luke had drawn the designs and oversaw the construction for both.

Levi and Ellen, Anna's parents, were sitting and reading in the study as Anna opened the door. Fred held the door open as they entered the foyer. As they entered the room, Levi stood and smiled at the couple. He had known Fred and his dad for years. He extended his hand to Fred and said, "Was it worth a dip in the pool to have a date with Anna?"

Fred, a little embarrassed, looked at Anna.

Anna shrugged her shoulders and said, "I did not tell them. Aunt Maddie told Mom."

Fred nodded and smiled at Anna, "Oh yeah. It was worth it."

Everyone laughed as Anna put her hand in his and rewarded him with a smile.

Ellen had cookies and drinks for the kids,

and after serving, she and Levi were getting ready to go upstairs to bed. Anna began showing the house to Fred. As they walked around the study, Anna pointed out pictures and told him about Grandpa August and Molly, who were still pastoring a good sized church in Paris, Arkansas.

She showed pictures of her dad and Uncle Luke in World War One, and then of the early days in the air mail service. She showed him pictures of the air transport days and then of the pictures when the two couples went to Hollywood at the invitation of Robert Allen, the producer.

"Why, that is Clark Gable standing with your dad and mom, and your aunt and uncle! I recognize several other movie stars as well!"

"It was no big thing. Dad and Uncle Luke flew as stunt pilots in a couple of movies. Although, Aunt Maddie <u>did</u> do a little wing walking in one."

"Wow! I am impressed! You must get your crazy ways from your Aunt Maddie!"

"I am afraid she does, Fred. I am so much afraid of heights," smiled Ellen, Anna's mom.

"We are going to be friends then, Mrs. Johnson. I am afraid of the Ferris Wheel at the fair!" Everyone laughed.

The Johnsons said good night, and Anna and Fred took their drinks out beside the pool and sat on the double swing on the patio. They had known one another for years, but both were a little shy toward one another as they talked and looked for parameters for their new relationship. Both were wondering where they were to go from there.

Anna put her head over on Fred's shoulder as he put his arm around her.

"You know, Fred, this just seems right somehow. I have known you since grade school, but I never dreamed you liked me too."

"Anna, you have thrown me into a swimming pool, and when we were younger you threw sand on me from the playground. You must have liked me a lot for a long time for you to be so mean to me! You must have known I liked you too."

"I guess I did, but I could just not get you to do anything about it. So, I am sorry, but when the opportunity came, I took matters into my own hands."

Fred kissed her quickly and said softly, "Well, I am glad you did."

"Listen, Anna, would you like to go to the Travelers game tomorrow afternoon? They are playing some team from Texas which is supposed to be pretty good."

"Sure! I have not been this summer. What time are you picking me up?"

"Game starts at one, but let's go early enough to watch batting practice. Say I pick you up at eleven thirty and we can eat something before we go."

"Great. I will be looking forward to it."

The Little Rock Travelers were a minor league baseball team which played in the old Texas League at Ray Winder Field which was built in 1931. It was a highlight of the Summer for nearly everyone both young and old to get to go and experience baseball at its best, complete with hotdogs and the sounds of the fans.

Anna walked Fred to his car holding hands and kissed him as if her mother was watching, because she knew she was. It was still enough to make them feel warm, and Anna held him with her head on his chest for a moment before she let him go.

"Good night, Fred. I enjoyed it."

"Me too. Tomorrow can not get here fast enough!"

Anna's mother smiled at her as she came into the house. Anna hugged her mom and told her, "He is really nice, Mom. He treats me like a queen."

"He knows if he doesn't you will throw him back into the pool!"

They both laughed, and walked with their arms around one another as they went up the stairs to their bedrooms. Once she was in her room, Anna looked at an old photograph from grade school with her and Fred and some of her other friends. She smiled, and for a moment she was in braces in the 6th grade. She knew Fred liked her and had kept the picture in her scrapbook. Beside the photograph were the words in her grade school cursive; "Fred Tanner likes me!" She hugged the scrapbook to her chest after closing and smiled just before turning off the lamp beside her bed.

Chapter Three

The three couples started being seen together every day in some way. They went to see the Travs play, went swimming at Rockaway Beach, some nights on the weekends they went to the Asher Drive In Movie, and nearly at least one meal a day was spent at Pete's Drive In.

The group was sitting at the drive in under the canopy with Austin, Mallory, Anna, and Fred in Austin's car with the top down. James and Payton were in his car beside them also with the top down. Jill, the blonde, pretty carhop, who flirted with Austin just to irritate Anna, had already brought hamburgers and drinks.

"Austin, when are you heading for the University?" asked Fred.

He and Austin were going to be roommates. It would give Anna a chance to be around both of her favorite men at the same time.

"We have to be there on Monday the 12th of August for the start of football two a days. So, I guess I will drive up on Saturday. How about you?"

"Yes, of course. If you want, we can travel together. Anna says she is riding up with me. She has to be there to practice cheerleading."

"Well, if the school would let Freshman

women have cars on campus the way that guys get to, I could drive myself. I even <u>have</u> to live in the dorm. Not fun. I will probably get some loser for a roomie."

"I feel sorry for whoever gets you!" kidded Austin.

"Mallory, slap him for me. I can't reach him!" They all laughed.

"Besides, you don't even have a car."

"Well, I am looking, and taking my time. My family has several cars and if I need to borrow one they are available."

"What would you really like to have?"

Anna looked pensive for a moment as if she was wondering should she tell them the truth. She looked at Fred and then Austin.

"Believe it or not, I would like a new 1940

67

Ford Woody Station Wagon. When I went with my folks to New Hampshire last winter to go skiing, the hotel owner picked us up and all our luggage in one. There was room for people plus all their luggage. It was the neatest thing.

Then, when we all went to California last summer, some of the kids were driving older woody station wagons to carry their surfing paraphernalia. Okay, you asked, and I told you the truth."

"Anna, I think that would be a perfect car for you, especially as much as you like to camp and picnic with your friends. Don't look at me like that, for once I am being serious with you!"

Anna smiled at him in appreciation.

"Well, we better get home," she said, "We

are eating at your house tonight and I want to clean up first. So, if you don't care, Austin, take Fred and me to my house. His car is over there for some reason. My dad is thinking about adding on to the garage to give him a stall of his own." Anna smiled at Fred and patted his knee, when everyone laughed at him.

"We are eating at six," said Austin, "and you know how John and Lydia like for everyone to be exactly on time. Sometimes I forget they are not really family, but they are so much a part of the Johnson household they may as well be."

"How did they come to be at your house?" asked Fred.

"It is a long, but great story. I will ask John to tell you sometime."

The meal of fried chicken, rice, egg rolls, and salads was served outside, and afterward everyone was sitting and visiting. John and Lydia joined them after making sure everyone was served. Fred told John he was interested in hearing his life story. John and his wife looked at one another, and Lydia spoke quietly, "It is up to you, but everyone loves to hear it because it shows sometimes God blesses us in unexpected ways."

"Well," said John in a measured voice as if he were picking his words carefully. "You may or may not know China was ruled for centuries by dynasties of emperors and one of the final dynasties was the Xing Dynasty. China at that point was even ruled by two women, Empress Dowager Ci'an and Empress Dowager Cixi.

The most ambitious was Empress Dowager Cixi.

She had been taken to the Emperor's court as a concubine at the age of 15. She passed her audition and was added to the Emperor's harem.

She began way down the "pecking order" on the princess line, but by having a son by the then emperor which she named Tongzhi she became an empress. Although he was only half legitimate, it was enough to ensure her presence in the palace. He became Emperor at the age of 18, but had been trained since he was 5 years old. However, Tongzhi died without a male heir which created a crisis in the succession of the dynastic line.

After great disagreement between the two

dowagers, they finally agreed upon Zaitian who was the first born of First Prince Chun Yixuan and Cixi's sister. He addressed Ci'an as "Huang O'niang" (Empress Mother) and Cixi as "Qin Baba" or (Biological Dad) to reinforce the image of her as the fatherly power figure.

Empress Ci'an died, after a short illness, of smallpox in April 1881. Ci'an's death meant the balance of power was now in Empress Cixi's favor.

Prince Gong, a warrior prince and once a favorite of Cixi, was a strong leader and struggled to gain more power, but Cixi downgraded his position to "advisor" and promoted the more loyal Chun to President of the Navy and the Army. Prince Chun, in what looked like a move of great loyalty, took funds from the military and began to reconstruct the Imperial Summer Palace outside of Beijing, which the invading Russians had burned, for the retirement of Cixi. Prince Chun in reality did not want Cixi to interfere with the young Guangxu's rule once he became of age.

My father, Langxu, was Chun's second born and was born just outside Beijing in 1875. As was the custom of the time, lesser born nobility were sent to America and other countries to study abroad. My father was trained in English and mathematics at Stanford University in California. He met a beautiful San Francisco socialite in college by the name of Louise Hearst who was a distant relative of Randolph Hearst. He wanted to marry her, but to do so meant he had to give up everything in

Chinese nobility.

The Empress Dowager Cixi did not really care because it meant her position and power was even more solid with him removed as a possible threat. In an unprecedented show of generosity, she gave him a wedding present of over a million dollars American in cash, plus quite a bit in stocks and bonds.

You can imagine what a 25 year old millionaire acquired in scurrilous friends from the Hearst family and other deceitful people. They lived very well for the time in San Francisco, and then moved to the Los Angeles and notably Monterey, California, area.

My father was very naïve, and lost most of his money by trusting this group of people which made a living, and their fortunes, from conning and cheating people.

I was born in 1898 and was already in college at UCLA when my mother went back to her people in San Francisco. My father went back to China and was heralded as a long lost son returning from a far country. He was loved and accepted all over again as the brother of the new Emperor. He died a few years later and was given a funeral ceremony as befitted a nobleman. He was buried by the time I found out, and I might not have gone back to China anyway.

I already had some money coming in from a trust fund to go to school, plus, I found I loved to cook, and took a part time job in a nice restaurant for extra money. I was only interested in martial arts, which is fairly nonexistent in America, and the job gave me something to do when not in school.

I met Miss Lydia in one of my philosophy classes. We were antagonists at first in most debates. I was from the Chinese culture and was very conservative. She was, and still is, a Progressive or a Socialist.

You know the scenario. What started as a war of words, grew into respect, then friendship, and finally I shocked all my friends by asking her to marry me!"

"Well how did you meet Mr. Johnson?"

"He and Miss Maddie loved to come to the upscale restaurant where I worked, whenever they were in Los Angeles. They kept sending very generous tips back to the Chef, which was me. So, after a few times, whenever they came to the restaurant, they would ask for me and I would come out personally and take their order. My manager did not mind at all. Luke Johnson tipped and paid <u>very</u> well!"

Everyone smiled and looked at Luke.

"What can I say? He was the best, and still is, chef I have ever met."

Everyone nodded their head and murmured agreement.

"Okay, but how did you become friends?" asked Fred.

"Let me answer this," smiled Luke.

"One night Maddie and I had stayed very late visiting with friends and business associates and the restaurant was already closed by the time we left. John saw us and waved. We offered him a ride. He started walking and talking with us on our way to our car. He asked how we liked his signature dish, Beijing Chicken a'la John Wong. We were still talking when we were approached by four men in the empty parking lot.

'Give me all your money, pretty boy!' One of them said. When I said, 'no!', he looked at the others and laughed. 'Well I guess we will just have to <u>take</u> it!'

'You might want to pack a lunch, there is only 4 of you and there are two of us,' I said.

'I think a pampered Pretty Boy and a little Chinaman we can handle. Besides, I have a knife!' he said, very cocky and self-assured.

'Let's <u>see</u> it!' spoke up John about that time. I am thinking, 'John stay out of this. I can handle it!'

The guy put out his hand and pushed the button on a switchblade knife. By the time the blade clicked fully open, John had grabbed the man's wrist, twisted it, took the knife away, and elbowed him in the face breaking his front teeth and causing blood to flow everywhere! He was knocked backward from the blow and was about 3 paces away holding his bleeding mouth. John whirled around so fast he was a blur, and kicked the man in the chest. He went flying back and was caught in the arms of his three friends. He was out cold!

I don't know who was more surprised, the 4 guys or me! Here stood this little, five foot five Chinese Chef, no offense, John, still in uniform holding the man's switchblade and asking if they still wanted our money.

The men picked up their friend and went running off looking over their shoulders to make sure he did not follow them! Their eyes were wide open in fear and astonishment! John looked at me, I looked at Maddie, and I looked back at John, and said, 'So, <u>that</u> is what they mean by Kung Fu!' John quietly bowed a little bow."

John took over the narrative.

"Maddie and Luke gave me a ride back to the nice hotel where Lydia and I lived. I did not have a car or a license, and all the cabs had pretty much quit running by that time at night. Today, they run all the time. Anyway, we sat and visited in the lobby with Lydia, who had come down from our apartment, and we decided to go back to Little Rock together.

Lydia could not have kids from a childhood illness, Austin and James were very young, and they needed someone to help take care of this huge house. So, here we are!"

"What a story!" exclaimed Fred. "So, that is where Anna and the guys picked up Kung Fu...from you!"

"Actually, as the son of nobility, I was taught Washu, which is lot more potent form of Kung Fu. I am also expert with sticks and double knives. In Chinese military, the nobility leads the men into battle. We have to know how to protect ourselves."

"I learned my lesson in Washu from Anna!"

Everyone laughed as Fred smiled at Anna.

As the party ended, the Potter sisters, Payton and Mallory, and Fred, now

81

understood why even as "masters of the manor" the children joined in helping John and Lydia clean up and pick up.

"I am impressed how your folks have taught you how to clean after a meal," said Fred to Anna and Austin. They both laughed out loud.

"John taught us, and mostly by example. We thought if a noble Chinese prince could clean, we could too. We have never questioned the practice. It makes his job easier."

"Your family is something special, Anna!" smiled Fred.

Anna walked Fred to his car. At his car Fred put his arms around her as she leaned against the driver's side door. The warm Arkansas night surrounded them with the sound of crickets and the flashing of fireflies. Anna put her head on Fred's chest after they kissed and held him tight.

"You smell better, Anna, than the honeysuckles and Magnolia blossoms!"

"Wow, look at you! My big football player is turning into a romantic! Next thing you will be spouting poetry!"

"I have never felt this way about anyone. For now, would you go steady with me?"

She raised her face up to him and said softly, "We <u>are</u> going steady, Fred. There's no one else for me either."

She kissed him again.

Austin and Mallory went for a drive along the Arkansas River and parked overlooking the slow moving current.

"I thought you might want to watch the submarine races, Mallory."

Caught off guard for just a moment, she squinted her eyes and looked at the river. "What? I don't see anything."

Austin smiled but wanted to see just how far she would go before she caught on.

"Look, the red one is passing the yellow one!"

Mallory looked one more time before Austin burst out laughing.

"Mallory, they are <u>submarines.</u> They are under the water. You can't see them!"

"So you were funning me the whole time? I was wondering why I could not see them!"

Austin by then was nearly hysterical with laughter.

Mallory frowned and said, "Well, I don't think it is that funny!"

"Actually, I just wanted to bring you up here to go parking."

"Why didn't you just say so? It's okay by me!"

She put her arms around his neck. After a moment of very passionate kissing, he pushed her back and whispered, "Mallory, we can't. I do care for you, but I am going to be leaving in a few days. I am not going to be just a summer lover. Let's just enjoy the moment together, and see how we feel after you go to school for your Senior year."

She looked him in the eyes for a moment.

"Thank you, Austin. I am still a virgin and I confess my first time could have been with you tonight."

She kissed him sweetly on the lips and said, "I don't know where she is right now, but there is a woman somewhere that does not know she is going to meet a dreamboat named Austin Johnson!"

"You know, Mallory, the same goes for you. I am not what you need right now. You need consistency and a long term relationship, and I just cannot give it to you. Do you understand this is not rejection, but a declaration of how much I care and respect you?"

She shook her head up and down yes. As Austin drove her home with her head on his shoulder, he did not notice the tears.

Chapter Four

L uke and Levi Johnson's birthday was on Monday, August 5th, in 1940. Because they were to turn 50, Maddie and the family were planning to have his huge party at the Little Rock Country Club. What started as a party with just a few close friends, turned into a happening with even several movie star friends wanting to attend. Robert Allen and Lela Mae also sent word they were coming. With all the celebrities coming, the guest list had swelled to well over three hundred!

Luke took John Wong, Austin and James

with him to purchase each a new tuxedo. Levi was meeting them from his workplace, the *Arkansas Gazette Newspaper*, where he was the Senior Editor. They went to a small, family specialty clothing store called Lou Hoffman's. All three men were trying on formal wear when Luke stood looking at himself in the three way mirror. Levi walked up behind him and stood smiling.

"Do you remember when Pop was getting married to Molly, and we drove up to Fort Smith to buy all of us new suits? We never saw him laugh and smile as much as we all did on that trip."

"You know, Levi, I am really a private person. These sort of things make me nervous. I wish Maddie and my family would have just given us a private little party."

"Actually, that was the way we started out, but after we invited one friend we could not stop! Who do you <u>not</u> invite? Face it, Luke, you and I have a lot of friends from our glory days at the University of Arkansas, the fighter squadron in World War I, the mail and passenger air lines, the movies, the architect and building business, not to mention the people we have met here at the Country Club.

You are a good, honest family man and businessman, fun to be around, and every one that meets you goes away thinking they are your best friend. Face it, Luke, no one at this party will do anything but wish you the best."

"You're right, I guess. That is why they call you the smart one!"

They both laughed at the old, private joke, and Levi patted Luke on the back.

"There you go, my brother. I am proud to be your brother. Besides, YOUR birthday is MINE!"

They both laughed. Austin said, "See? You really <u>are</u> smarter than me! I forgot we are twins!"

The Country Club had two huge dance floors, and both were filled the night of Luke's party. The one inside the ballroom was filled with more of the older guests there to hear the celebrities sing and dance to the orchestra. The dance floor outside by the huge pool was more youthful in decorations, guests, and the music, instead of an orchestra, was a "swing band."

Inside, while the older folks did the waltz, the guests outside were doing the hop and the jitterbug. The distinctive music and festivities between the two dance floors made Levi make an observation.

"Every generation seems to be defined by their music. It is widening the generation gap even more by polarizing the youth and their music from the older folks and their music."

"Well, I don't want to be a fuddy duddy, and so, I think I will go out and dance to the band for a while instead of the orchestra. How about you, Mr. Fred Astaire? I am not Ginger Rogers, but I am not afraid to try!"

After only a moment or two on the dance floor, the two were alone as Maddie danced with arguably the most influential modern dancer that ever lived. Maddie did very well even though, in all fairness, the dance steps were kept simple for her. There were lots of whirling and Maddie holding Mr. Astaire's hand while he did the showy dance steps. Afterward, he escorted her back to the table, and bowed to her to a thunderous round of applause.

It was a loud, festive affair. With all the celebrities and distinguished guests attending, even the radio stations from around the country were present!

Sitting at the Guest of Honor table were several celebrities including Clark Gable, Carole Lombard, and others. Maddie got a nice smile and wink from Clark, and lots of eyebrows went up, and Maddie just laughed.

She, Clark, and most importantly, Luke, knew they were just friends.

With Levi and several of his reporters present, the *Arkansas Gazette* carried the account of the party on the front page the next day. It even showed Maddie and Fred Astaire dancing.

Fred Tanner and Anna danced to Duke Ellington. Everyone wanted to see the new dances and new steps. Other "swing bands" included the bands of Glenn Miller, Tommy and Jimmy Dorsey, and even Louis Armstrong stood and played.

There was so much laughter coming from the main ballroom, when the band took a break, everyone went inside to listen. It was a small group of Jewish "Catskill comics" which included George Burns, Rodney Dangerfield, Jack Benny, Don Rickles, and more.

The jokes came one after another as the comedians stood in a line on the platform..

"I just got back from a pleasure trip," said one, "I took my mother-in-law to the airport!"

When the laughter died down enough to hear, another comedian said sadly, "I took my wife to the same hotel where we spent our wedding night. Only this time I stayed in the bathroom and cried!"

"We always hold hands when we go out. If I let go, she shops!"

"She was at the beauty shop for two hours. That was just for the estimate. She got a mudpack and looked great for two days. Then the mud fell off!"

A drunk was in front of the judge. The judge says, "You have been brought here for drinking. The drunk says, "Great, let's get started!"

Each comedian took his turn to amuse the crowd. Even though a lot of greats were present, Luke still received a tremendous round of applause when introduced as the Birthday Boy. The cake was six feet tall and lit by 50 candles. Everyone received at least a small piece.

Later, at home with several friends sitting by the pool, Luke stood and clicked a spoon against his water glass.

"One is a very rich man to have this many friends. I thank you from the bottom of my heart for making this such a special day.

Thanks to my wife and family, I will cherish this memory as long as I live."

Luke sat down quickly, but everyone saw him misting up from emotion. He could no longer speak. He pointed to Levi and nodded for him to say something. There were several people dabbing at their eyes with handkerchiefs.

Levi stood and in almost a solemn voice looked at Luke and said, "I have always enjoyed being the "lesser" brother. No, I mean it! Luke is one of the best people I have ever met. His integrity, courage, and intelligence are unlike anyone I have ever met."

Robert Allen laughed, "We are not going to start singing and have a group hug are we?"

They all laughed and gathered around the

two men to shake hands and pat them on the back.

Richard Allen and Lela Mae spent the night with Luke and Maddie, and Levi and Ellen joined them as they sat up and talked until the sun just started to lighten the Eastern sky.

"You know, thanks for everything, Richard. Our lives would have been totally different without you. I am proud you are my friend."

Richard stood and shook hands and then hugged him.

"Do you want to go steady?"

They all laughed out loud.

At the airport the next day, everyone shook hands with celebrities as well as family members which had traveled to the party. The newspaper again reported on the event as well as took dozens of pictures.

The Luke and Levi Johnson 50th Birthday Party of 1940 was talked about for years at the Country Club..

Chapter Five

The trip a week later to Fayetteville and the University of Arkansas was like a family outing. Mallory rode with Austin and Luke, Maddie, Levi, and Ellen all went in Luke's big Cadillac. James and Payton went in his car, and Anna rode with Fred. Mallory's parents, had told their farewells back in Little Rock, and she and her twin sister, Payton, would ride back to Little Rock with James.

Once in the dorm, Anna and Austin waited an embarrassing few moments while their mothers made their beds. It was even worse when they got ready to leave when their parents gave them hugs and kisses.

"Aw, Mom," whined Austin. "It's not like we are leaving home. We will be home every long holiday and weekend. Besides, if we really had to see you, Dad can come up in our plane."

"Austin, it is not <u>you</u> I am worried about. It is <u>me</u> missing you!"

Austin put his arms around his mother and held her for a moment while she lay her head on his chest.

"Mom, this should be the best part of your life. It is like making a kite and then see if it is going to fly, and how well is it going to fly."

"You are right, Austin. You are going to do well in life. I am already proud of you, and when it comes James' turn to leave, he will do well too. But, I am a mom and I still hate letting go of my little boys!"

Austin hugged her tight and just shook his head, because he knew she was right, and this was hard on her. He could be embarrassed for her show of affection, but he loved his mother.

Austin, Anna, and Fred stood by the Spoofer's Stone on the quad and watched as everyone loaded and waved goodbye to their family. It was touching but they were ready to start their college careers.

"Well, needless to say, but you guys did okay on your roommates, but I wonder what I'll get. I saw her name on the door, and she is from Alabama. She must be a cheerleader too to be coming early, but she went to high school in Birmingham at a private school for girls. I am sure she is going to be a snob."

"You are prejudging someone you have never met. You can do better than that, Anna. You are almost a socialist you want to have everyone treated fairly and equally," said Fred.

"Fred's right, Anna. Give her the benefit of the doubt. At least wait and meet her."

"Her name is listed on the door as Elizabeth Ann Davis, and in parenthesis is (Beth Ann). Let's go over to the girl's dorm and see if she is here yet."

The threesome walked along the sidewalk and read the names on the bricks. Every year each Senior had his name put on the walk. It had been going on since 1876.

"Look!" exclaimed Anna, "There's dad and

Uncle Luke's names! Class of 1911 for their undergraduate degrees, and Class of 1912 for their Master's! And there is Mom's name, Class of 1912!"

"Wait until you go to the gym and see my dad's name along with your dad's on the trophy for going undefeated in 1909 and winning the conference with a single defeat in 1910! Plus, dad was All-Conference in boxing! Seeing all this and knowing they walked this same campus makes me feel right at home! What about you, Fred?"

"My dad came for two years and then went back to Little Rock to help his dad open another grocery store. I am still very proud of him. He and his family own stores all over Little Rock, North Little Rock, and Hot

Springs. My dad made it all happen. His dad died not long after he came home, but he had time to teach him the business and he has done well."

Anna put her hand in Fred's, smiled at him, and said, "He did well!" Then she kissed him quickly on the cheek.

"Public displays of affection are not allowed on campus, young lady!"

All three turned to see a woman dressed in gray and beige clothing. She could have been forty years old, or sixty, or even thirty, but she had a very commanding presence with a dour frown on her face. A middle-aged black man, with "salt and pepper" hair in a dark suit, was struggling under a huge armload of suitcases, hat boxes, and vanity cases and was sweating while standing behind her. A smaller and younger version of the woman with similar hairdo and colored clothing was standing along side him while the mother had stepped forward to address Anna.

"Or what?" said Anna, and took a step toward her. Her eyes widened as Austin stepped between the two women. She was not used to people confronting her. He knew the woman at best was going to receive the first and worst tongue-lashing she had ever received, and at the worst....his mind reviewed and was alarmed at the possible havoc an out of control Anna might wreak on her. He tried to diffuse the situation.

"Look, Mam, we have only been here for a few hours. We should have read the part about kissing in public in our handbook. Although I have to admit I have seen others kissing and holding hands too. It obviously offends you and your husband, and we apologize."

The man with the luggage smiled behind her back and then quickly wiped it off.

"I am not married. This man is not my husband! Did you not notice he is black?"

"That is going on a lot these days. Most people <u>we</u> know are married though."

"You simpleton! This man is my chauffeur!"

"My mistake, mam. I apologize. Excuse us we are on our way to the new Freshman Girl's Dorm to visit my cousin's room." Austin smiled. He had been "putting her on" the entire time.

The woman sniffed, put her nose up in the air, turned around, and said sharply, "Samuel, get those bags up to Beth Ann's room and come back and get the others! Now!"

Anna looked at the girl and said, "I don't suppose your last name is anything but Davis, is it?"

The woman spoke again in a very impatient tone, "Yes, it is Davis! Why is that important to you?"

"Well, there is a Beth Ann Davis which was supposed to be coming today. She is a Freshman, and she is from Birmingham, Alabama. We were going to be roommates, but I am sure you can find another room."

"Why should we move?" the woman asked very haughtily.

Anna looked the lady right in the eyes and said, "First, I am already moved in with the bed made and everything of mine on my half of that room. Second, my clothes are in the closet and put up. I am <u>not</u> moving, and it is not open for discussion!"

Anna stepped around the woman and looking at the girl who had not said a word yet, smiled a little smile, and said, "She doesn't let you talk much, does she?"

The girl smiled timidly at Anna, glanced at her mother, and said, "I don't have to talk much. She speaks for all of us."

Her mother frowned and started walking toward the limousine. She looked over her shoulder at her daughter and Anna, stopped and turned all the way around to face them, and said with a little smile, "I know we do not agree on some things, Beth Ann, and coming all the way to Arkansas when we have great schools in Alabama is your way of getting away from me. However, I do want the best for you. I hope you are happy here."

She walked back toward the girls to within a couple of steps and smiled a surprisingly warm smile at Anna and said, "You will take good care of my baby girl, will you not? She is all I have."

Mrs. Davis stuck out her hand to Anna. She took her hand and before the lady could do anything, Anna hugged her briefly.

"We will be okay, Mrs. Davis. I promise. Stay in touch, and do not worry about her."

Tears began to well up in the lady's eyes.

"Thank you, Anna. I'm so glad she has a friend like you, and I know I was somewhat harsh before. I am sorry."

Then, to everyone's amazement she hugged Beth Ann and pulled Anna to her too! She turned away quickly as if a "public display of affection" embarrassed her. Also, she did not want anyone to see her cry. She waved from the open window on the limousine as they pulled away from the curb leaving Beth Ann's luggage. The girls and the guys all waved as she drove off.

Fred, Austin, and Anna helped Beth Ann carry her luggage up to her room, and in just a few moments the bed was made and clothes put away.

"Go with us, Beth Ann. We were just going

to eat. I'll even buy!" smiled Austin. Seeing the slight blush on Beth Ann's face, made Anna smile a little smile to herself.

"My Cuz!" she thought to herself.

By Monday morning Beth Ann was part of their group. Austin and Beth Ann even held hands coming home on Sunday evening after church. The two couples sat in the lobby of the girl's dorm and visited until the lights were dimmed which signaled it was time for all male visitors to leave. This time the guys hugged the girls, and managed a quick peck on the cheek before they left for their own dorm.

The house mother was standing with crossed arms watching, and she cleared her throat. Austin winked at her. She actually flushed a little from not being used to having young men wink at her with the audacity or good looks of Austin Johnson, but they left quickly. They did not want yet another confrontation over public displays of affection.

After the boys left, Anna and Beth Ann washed their faces and hands, removed what little makeup they wore, and put on their pajamas. They decided to sit up and visit. The girls were sitting on their beds with their legs folded under them. The first topic was about Austin, and was brought up by Beth Ann.

"Austin is quite a guy, isn't he? I have been around a lot of quality guys, but he is the finest I have ever met. Don't look at me like that, because I know he is probably not ready for more than just friends."

"Hey, you are really wise. All the girls love Austin, but he is complicated. He really has never fallen for anyone. Not that you're not, but she will have to be something special. You give him space and time and, who knows? We best be getting some sleep. Tomorrow is the first day of cheerleading!"

"Good night, Anna. I am glad I have you for a roomie. I was not sure what I might have. You will do til I find a better one!"

Beth Ann giggled, and Anna threw a small pillow at her and they both laughed.

"You are okay too. Good night."

Fred had been a favorite target as an offensive end for Austin in high school, and both were looking forward to playing together.

They were part of the team and were dressed out and on the field by seven to take advantage of the cooler temperature for the first practice.

The Arkansas Razorbacks played their games in 1940 in Razorback Stadium which was constructed in 1938. It did not have lights at first, and all the games had to be day games.

At the first practice, Coach Fred Thomsen had everyone run for time in the 100 yard dash. Austin and a Senior named George Talbert tied for the fastest on the team. They lined up on the goal line and three of them threw the ball to see who could throw it the farthest. Austin threw the ball from the goal line to the 20 yard line. It was a throw of 80 yards in the air. George could only manage a 65 yard throw. The third could only manage 55 yards, and the coach and the team were starting to like what they saw.

Fred Tanner was just a couple of steps behind Austin and George and was two inches taller and 20 pounds heavier than either. When the team moved to the hitting drills, it was apparent both Fred and Austin were used to going both ways, defense and offense, and knew what to do.

After a few minutes of contact drills, they started lining up in positions, and because Austin and Fred were Freshmen, they were put on the second team.

The coach walked them through the few basic plays they ran, and was all smiles as he blew the whistle and sent them to the showers. He thought the team looked the best for the first practice of any team he had ever had. As Austin and Fred walked out of the gym locker room, the coach came up to Austin and shook his hand.

"So, you are Luke Johnson's son. I heard about him and his brother, Levi, on the undefeated season team in 1909, and the next year when they lost only one game. He was a great player!"

"Thank you, sir!"

"Don't thank me yet. You have some high expectations to fulfill!"

"I am sure I do, but I can handle it."

The coach gazed at him for a moment, smiled, and said, "Just like your old man. He backed up his big talk though with a big walk.

I am glad to have you, Austin. I want to meet your dad if he comes up. Okay?"

Austin smiled and said, "I would not have ever been allowed to go anywhere else!" They both laughed. "You will like my dad."

After several days of "two a days" the coach wanted to have a little scrimmage with the first team against the second team. In 1940, before the modern "platoon" system, most players went both ways, and played offense and defense. Austin was the quarterback on offense and linebacker on defense for the second team.

The kickoff was first team to the second team to show them how to do it. The ball was placed on the 40 yard line, and when it was kicked, Austin handled the ball. He took the ball and made a couple of steps as if he were going to the left, but reversed his field, and, with a good block from Fred, he outran everyone to the end zone.

With all the interest in the new team, the stands had dozens of spectators. They went wild cheering on the Freshmen, who never had scored much in the past.

The kicker for extra points was Austin who drop-kicked the ball through the uprights which were placed on the goal line, and without running an offensive play, the second team was ahead 7-0.

"Your turn, Talbert. Let's see what you can do!" taunted Austin.

"You were just lucky, Johnson. We are going to run you off the field!"

"You gotta catch me first."

"We can do that!"

The coach smiled as they lined up for the kickoff. He thought to himself, "This should be interesting."

Fred punted the ball instead of using the tee. The ball went over 55 yards in the air, and when it finally came down, George had just put it under his arm when something which felt similar to a truck hit him so hard he almost lost consciousness, but, worst of all, the ball came loose and Fred covered it. George groaned as he tried to clear his head, and Austin patted him on the chest as he pushed up off him.

"Get used to it, Talbert. It's going to be that way all day!"

After only about 30 minutes of playing, and the coach stopping once in a while to point something out or make a comment, the score was 28-0 for the second team. He blew his whistle and said, "That's it for today! Hit the showers!" He was smiling a very broad smile.

Austin caught up with George Talbert who was limping back to the locker room with his leather helmet in his hand. He patted him on the back and said, "It was not personal at all, George. It was just football. Are we still friends?"

"Of course we are. Anyone that can beat me around on a football field like you just did is my best friend! I am glad you are on my side. Come on, I'll buy you a Coke."

Austin, George, and Fred Tanner showered, dressed and went to The Little Pig Drive In. Austin and Fred went in Austin's car and George went in his 1937 Ford Rumble Seat Coupe. It was a tossup which was more fun; the convertible or the rumble seat. Both were very popular with the dating crowd, especially if one was taking his date to the Drive-In Movie or to the "submarine races."

The young men went inside and sat at a table with six chairs. They were getting ready to place their orders when a pretty, turquoise colored 1940 Dodge convertible drove up with a load of five University of Arkansas cheerleaders. Anna and Beth Ann were among the laughing group of girls.

"I knew we would find you guys here after practice!" beamed Anna. "Don't you <u>ever</u> get enough to eat?"

The guys laughed, and Austin said, "You know we always have room for a hamburger. Besides, we had our first scrimmage today, and we used up a lot of energy!"

"Yes, we know. It is all over campus the second team beat the first team! Oops, sorry George. I forgot you are on the first team," said Anna.

"No problem. We are all on the same team and that is all that matters. Your cousin is a great football player!"

"Yes, he is, and at least he is humble!" everyone laughed.

After they ate and visited for a while, George and Belinda, his fiancee, were getting ready to leave on their own. They were to get married when the school year was over. George was finishing a degree in accounting, and, having been in the Army ROTC program at the University of Arkansas for the last four years, he was taking Belinda to Washington D.C. after they were married. His dad was a Colonel in the Army and wanted his son to be on his staff. Colonel Talbert was a very influential person to know.

George got up and shook Austin's hand.

"You know registration begins this week. So, both of you meet me at the entrance to Old Main and I will help you guys get registered. I know all the teachers and can tell you the best ones to get."

"Why thank you, George," said Anna with a warm smile. "I am lost already about where to go."

"It won't take long to find your way around. If football players can do it, you can do it, Anna."

He smiled back, and Belinda took his hand quickly and said, "Come on, we better go!"

Austin smiled at Anna as the couple left.

"Quite a little troublemaker, aren't we?"

"Okay, she may not ever be my best friend, but I am not interested at all in trading in my man Fred."

She put her arm around him and smiled.

Chapter Six

Having a friend like the Senior, George Talbert, to help the group of Freshman find all their classes, and also help cut a few corners by knowing the enrolling process, was helpful, and everyone was ready for class to start the next day in only a few hours. Most everyone's classes were in the Old Main building, and it helped.

Anna was majoring in education to be a physical ed teacher back home in Little Rock. Austin and Fred both decided to major in Architecture like Austin's dad. He still owned a major firm in Little Rock, and he was excited his son would someday take it over.

Most of the young men had signed up for Army ROTC. They received uniforms and all immediately began marching all over campus to get used to the drills and cadence. Fred was shown by Austin how to keep their uniform creases razor sharp and his shoes were "spit shined" until they looked like patent leather. Both received outstanding in every personnel inspection.

The third week of school the week in ROTC was to be given to self defense training. They had all dressed in regulation workout sweatsuits, and Austin still managed to look neater than most of the other guys. A fatigue uniformed enlisted man from the Army by the name of Sergeant Zeke Warner was brought in to train them in hand to hand combat. Austin watched the man a few times as he threw the trainees around on the mat. After a while he had pretty well bruised most of the young men. He looked toward Austin and smiled a sinister grin.

"How about you, lady? You want to try me?"

"What are the rules? I am not going to let you work me over like you have these others. Am I allowed to defend myself?"

The Army non-com smiled and said, "You can do any thing you would like, but if I want to put you down, you will go down."

"Fair enough."

The two men circled one another warily.

The sergeant was surprised at the grace and speed of this Freshman. He passed off every opening feint that he made with ease. All the college men were yelling for Austin to pin him, and it was starting to irritate the man. He finally tried a leg whip to bring him down, but Austin stepped inside of his leg and grabbed him by the front of his shirt with one hand and flipped the man quickly over on his belly on the mat with the other, and had him in a choke grip before he could even defend himself. The grip around his throat by Austin's forearm and the pressure of his hand on the back of his head were causing him to start to lose consciousness.

"Okay! Okay! Release me! I must have slipped! Let's try it again and this time I won't be so nice!"

"Okay by me, sir. No broken bones or contusions will be the rules, but let's see something a little more special than what you have shown us so far."

The man flushed a dark red and said, "Why you insolent punk!"

He came at Austin in a run, but Austin sidestepped him and knelt on one knee for leverage and almost threw him off the mat on his back. Before he could do anything Austin had his leg held straight and was starting to bend it backwards. The pain from the stretching ligaments in his knee from just a little of Austin's pressure caused the man to yell.

"Don't break it! I give up!"

Austin rolled over like a cat and pushed himself off the mat in a flip to land on his feet. He smiled at the man who was holding his knee and whining. He extended his hand and offered to help him up, but the man slapped his hand away and yelled, "Class dismissed!"

Captain Barry Bucholz, the officer in charge of the ROTC program, smiled to himself. He had never liked Zeke, and had been watching the entire match from his office through a one way glass. Nearly every semester Zeke hurt someone by his bullying, but this time it was his turn. As the men filed by his office, he opened his door and said, "Johnson, may I speak with you?"

"Yes, Sir! Recruit Austin Johnson at your service, Sir!" He stood rigidly at attention looking straight ahead.

"At ease, recruit."

Austin immediately snapped to parade rest with his hands behind his back, and his head up looking the officer in the eyes.

There was a little twinkle in his eyes as he could see here was a class act. He had already bested his best man in hand to hand, and he had seen him run all over a football field as the team won 38-0 on the first weekend of the season.

"Where did you learn the Washu? I have only seen the nobles in China use that form of hand to hand."

"You are right, sir. We have a main man or butler, or whatever, from China which has been our caretaker for over 15 years. We have practiced every single day except Sunday since we were tots."

"I am impressed, Mr. Johnson. I will keep my eyes on you. You are an interesting young man."

"Thank you, sir. If I was out of line to Mr. Warner I will apologize to him."

"Between you and me it won't hurt him to be knocked down a notch. He can be heavy handed sometimes. I liked it!"

Officer Bucholz shook hands with him and dismissed him. Austin snapped to attention, saluted, and said, "Thank you, sir!"

As Austin left his office, Bucholz smiled at his gung ho attitude. He thought to himself how much he reminded him of his own youthful fervor. He would keep his eyes on him. Men like Austin Johnson did not come along very often.

Austin became mildly famous on campus after the incident in the self-defense class. Yet, even Anna remarked how unchanged he seemed to be. She had come to expect the unexpected with him. He was mysterious and self-contained. He was a man unto himself, and he acted like nothing special had happened.

The Arkansas Razorbacks were a very small team in 1940 compared to the other teams in the Southwestern Conference. Even with Austin playing his best, the team only went 4-6 with only one win in the conference in the season. With the war going on in Europe, already American young men in Arkansas were going off to the war in droves. They just could not compete with the teams from Texas with much larger enrollments. Austin and the rest of the team were just glad when the season was over.

Fred and Anna continued to date and started being alone more and more. Beth Ann told Anna she knew Austin in his own way liked her, but there was a part of him he continued to shield from her and the world. He was sure complicated just like Anna had commented. He was fun, good looking, talented, courteous, but she never felt they were connecting.

Austin went out with Beth Ann every weekend, and sometimes they hung out with Fred and Anna at the University Center. He never said they were going steady or anything, but no one else ever asked her out. She was content to see Austin and be seen with him.

As the weather turned colder in the Fall, all of the couples sat around the big fireplace in the University Center, or one of the dormitories talking and laughing. Once in a while someone would play a guitar or even a ukelele. There were lots of singing some nights until the house mother turned the lights down. She gave them an extra hour on the weekends. She never smiled at any other young man except Austin. She always stood by the door to lock it behind the men. He never failed to give her a quick hug and sometimes a peck on the cheek which invariably made her smile and even blush a little.

Anna and Beth Ann kidded him about something "going on" between the two, but Austin would just smile.

Chapter Seven

The University of Arkansas shut down the second week of December in 1940 for the Christmas or midyear break. Beth Ann and Austin went together to the train station for her to go home to Alabama for the holiday.

"Austin," began Beth Ann, "thank you for being my friend this semester. I enjoyed being thought of as your girl. It made me feel like I am somebody special."

"Beth Ann, you <u>are</u> somebody special. I am only 19, and I do not have a clue where I am going in life. I appreciate you not trying to put

137

reins on me."

Beth Ann smiled and put her arms around him, and held him tight. Very quietly and firmly she told him, "Austin, I am transferring to the University of Alabama in January. I won't be coming back even though it has been a very hard decision. My mother and I are communicating for the first time in our lives. She is not in good health and I am going back to Birmingham to watch over her while I am going to school. I don't expect you to even remember my name a year from now, but if you think of me, write me once in a while, and let me know what you are doing and where you are. Would you?"

"Yes, I will. Honestly, I don't know how often, but I will write at least occasionally, I promise."

"My mother is going to have a cow when she sees my short hair and new wardrobe! I thought rather than have her worry I would not tell her. I will just surprise her."

"Well, you look great, Beth Ann. I enjoyed taking you places."

They kissed for a long time, and she smiled at him and said, "I would get in trouble with Mother over that kiss, but it would be worth it!"

He watched her smile at him as she boarded the train. She found a seat so she could see him through the window. She blew one kiss at him, and then held her hand up with her palm out in goodbye until the train took her out of sight.

Austin drove home from school alone, and Fred and Anna traveled together in Fred's car. As he followed the couple down Highway 64 through Clarksville, Russellville, Morrilton, Conway, North Little Rock, and finally into Little Rock, Austin felt in a sober mood. He would miss Beth Ann for she understood he wanted his space and never seemed to question it. By the time they got to Little Rock and crossed the bridge over the Arkansas River, all of them were already looking forward to John's home cooking.

When Austin, Fred, and Anna left for school it was Summer, and now the lack of leaves on the gray trees coupled with the amber grass created a mood of melancholy which suddenly came over them as they turned off the highway and traveled up the drive.

They all smiled, however, at all the Christmas decorations. There were lights wrapped around the trees in the yard, and there was a huge tree shining through the windows as they approached the house. Suddenly the doors flew open and they heard James yell, "They're here!"

By the time the two cars stopped they were mobbed by family. James opened Anna's door and got a big hug for doing so. John and Lydia came, bowed, patted them, and told them how much they had been missed. Fred kissed Anna quickly on the lips and said his goodbye for he knew everyone was watching. Austin and

Anna's parents all came out to greet them, and they all waved at Fred as he left.

"Hey look! Even Grandpa August and Molly are here!" exclaimed Anna.

It was a joyous reunion. It had been several months since they had seen their grandparents, and all were excited.

August and Molly were driving a new Lincoln. August still had lots of hair, but it was no longer jet black. However, he was still strong looking. Molly colored her hair, but she looked beautiful and robust for a woman of 70. After embraces all around, everyone went inside to sit by the fire. John and Lydia served hot chocolate and coffee for everyone. Plus, Lydia had already made the first fruitcake of the season in which she used rum for seasoning.

Luke kidded her by saying, "You know, Lydia, this is wonderful, but you need to use more rum!"

Everyone laughed and Lydia replied, "You know one can not taste the rum after it is cooked. It only gives a pleasant aroma! I am not falling for that tease this year!"

After a huge meal and passing out gifts on Christmas Eve, everyone's conversations were on memories of Christmas past. The huge fireplace had stockings hung for every member of the families, including John and Lydia. Pine and cedar decorations were all over the room. The fresh scent reminded everyone it was Christmas.

On the mantle was an antique nativity scene which had been lovingly hand carved from wood by Norman and painted by Bonnie, Maddie's parents, which had died a few years before within just a few weeks of one another. Norman died first from a heart attack, and Bonnie could not live without him, and she had died from a flu attack brought on by not eating. Maddie could not get her mother to carry on her life without him.

On a lighter note, Luke kidded and reminded the blushing Maddie of the Christmas Levi proposed to Ellen, but she was not sure, and had even come home from college with another guy, Richard Allen, who now was an old family friend.

Maddie told the astonished Luke, "You

know, when I saw the ring you bought, if you had went ahead and asked, I would have said yes."

"Now you tell me! Maddie, look how many years we could have been together if we both had not been so stubborn! I was not going to go ahead and ask when you had just told me you were not sure. I did not want to be turned down in front of everybody."

Maddie put her arms around him and looked into his eyes as she said, "Luke, if it is any consolation, I never one time thought I did not love you. The money turned my head, for a while, but I did not want anyone, ever, except you."

"Good answer! Did you notice we are standing under the mistletoe? Come here, you!"

Luke held her off the ground for a moment as he kissed her. As he let her back down, he smiled with tears in his eyes, "Seems like old times, huh?"

"How about one more for <u>old</u> times?" Maddie smiled.

Chapter Eight

By mid January, after the Christmas and New Year Holidays, the school work began to settle into a routine, and Austin began to study very intensely. He missed Beth Ann, but he had plenty of women to choose from if he needed to have an escort. His Architecture degree plan required several Math and Physics courses, as well as English. There was plenty to keep him busy and his mind from women.

"You know, Austin, I am worried you are not having any fun," said a serious Anna. They were sitting in a booth at the University Center with Fred.

"Would you quit trying to run my life?" he smiled.

"I am only trying to help. However, my dad is flying the plane up this afternoon to pick Fred and me up to fly to Birmingham to see Beth Ann. Why don't you come with us? Her mother's funeral was just two days ago, and I am sure she could use the distraction too. We can stay at their big mansion. She called last night and she asked about you. I think she still likes you, and she sorta needs you."

Austin heaved a big sigh and said, "Okay. I would like to see Beth Ann too. I really have not found anyone yet to take her place."

"I don't want to hear <u>yet</u>. I think you liked

her more than you are letting on." When Anna smiled at him, he just shrugged his shoulders in answer and smiled.

"If I ever do have a wife I hope she does not nag like you do.!"

"If a woman doesn't nag, she doesn't love you. Don't you know that?"

Austin shook his head, looked at Fred, and said, "She's certifiable, you know that?"

"Don't get me in this. You are on your own. The last time I confronted her, I wound up in the pool! Actually, my friend, we just care about you."

"I know you do, but I am fine. I promise. I will go pack a suit, and an extra pair of socks for the trip."

Anna smiled and rolled her eyes at his

remark, however, she was glad she had got Austin to go with them. She believed it was best for all parties involved.

Levi and Ellen flew into the Fayetteville airport that afternoon around 2 p.m. They were in the Beechcraft twin engine plane belonging to the family. It was used for traveling back and forth to California for business mostly, but it had come in handy more than once to get people long distances in the shortest possible time. It had seats for eight not including the pilot and co-pilot.

All three were waiting at the airport with their bags. Ellen and Levi went to the restroom, the plane was refueled, and they flew from Fayetteville to Birmingham on a cloudless day.

There was a surprising amount of green

mixed in with the tan and brown of pastures and fields which were being prepared for planting. Austin sat in the co-pilot's seat, and even took the controls until they were preparing to land when Levi took over.

"Thanks, Uncle Levi. I have not been up for a while and I really have missed flying."

"It has been great for me too. Your dad and I never got enough except when someone was shooting at us." Levi smiled.

As the plane landed, the black, Lincoln limousine belonging to the Davis family was there. As the plane rolled to a stop and the steps were put into position, the door was opened by Samuel, the black chauffeur, looking impeccable as always. Beth Ann got out quickly and started running across the tarmac. By the time she got to the foot of the steps, Anna was there to hug her tight as they both stood and cried.

"Look who else is on the plane!"

Austin was standing in the doorway smiling. He took the steps two at a time and swept Beth Ann into his arms and lifted her off the ground as he hugged her. He kissed her quickly on the lips, but both realized they were not alone. He put her back down, but kept his arm around her.

"Somebody had to come and keep Anna out of trouble!" All laughed as she made a face at him.

"It seems as if we have not seen one another for months, instead of a few weeks, so much has happened!" exclaimed a tearful Beth

Ann. "I am so appreciative and glad you are here!"

Fred, Samuel, and Ellen's parents unloaded the luggage as Beth Ann walked between Anna and Austin arm in arm as they went on ahead to the limo. As the two girls got in, Austin helped load the final bags and sat beside Beth Ann. The big limousine held 6 comfortably, and though everyone was somewhat subdued because of the circumstances it was obvious the group was happy to be together again.

In the silence, Anna started talking first, "Beth Ann," as she leaned across and put her hand over hers, "I know this is the most trite question in the world, but are you okay?"

"Yes. Yes, I am. Mother and I sat and talked for hours. She had been so consumed with making a lady out of me she forgot to make a daughter out of me. Those were her words. We cried a lot because she knew she was very sick and was not going to see me finish growing up.

She told me you were such a fresh breath of air compared to all the little old biddies she knew, and she wanted me to be more like you. I needed to be able to stand on my own. She even confessed she loved my short hair and brighter clothes!"

"Good! I was so worried she would blame me for messing you up!" The two young women smiled at one another.

The Davis Estate was nearly as large as the Johnson's. The actual main house held the servants' quarters on one wing instead of behind the house as at Luke and Maddie's home. It did have a 4 car garage, and Beth Ann said all the servants had stayed. In fact, she thought they were probably glad to be treated with respect. The atmosphere itself was lighter and laughter was heard in the house for the first time in years.

"Mother was not as mean as everyone believed. She was afraid to let her guard down and thought she needed to be firm to run everything. Mother had been such a part of my father's publishing business for years, that when he died after a long illness, the leadership transfer was seamless."

The group was sitting in the library around a nice fire in big, overstuffed leather chairs. The two, pretty, light tan skinned servants,

Mattie and Hattie, their mother had been half black, came and went quietly as they served coffee and tea. Mattie had baked a cake and sweet rolls and everyone smiled and thanked the two women. Later, Mattie would tell Hattie how nice the visitors were. Most visitors treated them very indifferently, as if they were still slaves.

Austin had his arm around Beth Ann, and the two were sitting in a two place love seat, and he looked at her and said quietly, "What now? Can you run the family business?"

"No, I won't have to. It is a corporation, and my dad's brother, Uncle Jim, has been the CEO of it for the last few years and will take over for Mother. Daddy and Mother left 40 percent of the business to him. I have 52 percent, and the rest is owned by shareholders. It is doing well. I trust him, and even though I have had offers to sell, I want to someday run it. I am majoring in Business Management already. Speaking of which, I have a surprise for you. Would you let me fly back with you? I have already re-enrolled at the University of Arkansas and they even allowed me to continue to be Anna's roomie!"

Everyone was happy, and Anna squealed and jumped up and down at the thought of having her roommate back. Austin was smiling as if he were glad too.

Levi and Ellen were invited to sleep in the Master Bedroom downstairs and there were shared rooms for Fred and Austin, and Anna and Beth Ann.

The next morning Beth Ann, as was her usual custom, got up early and almost tiptoed to the kitchen to not awaken anyone. She heard laughter coming from the kitchen. She pushed open the swinging kitchen door and saw Austin visiting and laughing with Samuel, Hattie and Mattie.

"Oh, good morning! I hope we did not wake you. I was telling the girls how Anna threw Fred in the pool. We have a fresh pot of coffee going, want a cup?"

Hattie said, "I will get it for her. She likes a little cream in hers instead of black like you do, Mister Austin."

"I don't guess I ever thought you would be up early, Beth Ann. I was just making myself at home. I hope you don't mind. I used to get up

158

early every morning and drink coffee with my dad before the day started."

"That's funny. I used to do the same thing when my dad was alive and I was young."

Austin smiled at her and was thinking Beth Ann was no diva expecting breakfast in bed. He liked her more and more. Most of the girls he knew, which came from homes with money, were so spoiled he very seldom dated.

"Do you like cars? Let's go for a ride before everyone gets up."

"It is my one vice!" He smiled and said.

She shook her head and said, "Oh, really. One vice."

He smiled again and said, "Okay I guess I do like chocolate milk shakes. I am not perfect, am I?"

Beth Ann laughed, and though she was thinking he was pretty close to perfect, she said, "If those are the worse vices you have, we can make this friendship work!"

She put her arm through his as they walked out through the kitchen into the garage. There were several cars, including the limo under covers, but Austin saw a pair of huge looking headlights under one and when he pulled it back, he exclaimed, "Wow! That is a Duesenberg! I have wanted one since I was a kid! Can I drive?"

Beth Ann smiled at his antics around the dark red convertible.

"Men!" she thought to herself. The "dooozie" had been her dad's favorite car to take her for a ride. It brought back so many pleasant memories of happier times.

"Sure. Let me help take off the cover. "

Even before the cover was off, Samuel came in and helped get the car ready to drive. It was a little cool for the top down, but he started it and let it warm up for them. Austin and Beth Ann were all smiles as the heater warmed their toes as Austin slowly backed it out of the garage.

"You be careful with my baby! I mean BOTH of them!"

"Trust me, Mr. Samuel, <u>no</u> one could appreciate an automobile like this one more than me. By the way, I have a pilot's license."

Samuel laughed and said, "You may be glad you do when you open it up a little on the open road!"

The Duesenberg was capable of 140 mph. An unheard of number for its time. It was the first automobile in America with hydraulic brakes, and a host of other ingenious ideas, such as dashboard mounted lights to tell when to change oil (750 miles), a light for when to check the battery (1500 miles), and other inventions that cars only in the last few years have begun to emulate. The supercharged SJ model would run an eight second 0 to 60 with a top speed of 140. With a price tag of around 25,000. dollars, it was a very pricey toy for only the super rich. Gary Cooper, Clark Gable, Greta Garbo, and James Cagney were examples of Duesenberg customers.

After about an hour, everyone was standing on the porch and waving as Austin

162

and Beth Ann came driving slowly into the driveway. With the top down their hair was a little windblown, but they did not care. They had been for a drive in a Duesenberg!

Austin had several pictures taken of him and Beth Ann in and around the car. He knew no one back at school would believe he had driven such an icon of American conspicuous consumption. Doctors and lawyers were making 3 to 5 thousand dollars a year. Austin told himself he could never justify owning a Duesenberg. He was indeed a multimillionaire, but public scorn and opinion would just be too much for him to deal with at his age. For the moment he had driven his dream car, which was enough.

On the trip back to Fayetteville, Beth Ann

took a nap with her head on Austin's shoulder. Every time he looked at Anna, she was smiling. He stuck out his tongue at her, but he was smiling too.

After moving Beth Ann back into the room with Anna, things got back to normal chaos at school. Everyone studied hard, but there were numerous good times of dating, walking to class, attending basketball games, and as the weather warmed going into Spring, the foursome would go on long drives into the Ozark Mountains.

One weekend they surprised August and Molly by driving up unannounced. Austin was concerned he was falling in love for the first time in his life. While Molly, Anna and Beth Ann were preparing a meal, Fred sat in a rocking chair on the porch. Austin and his grandfather went for a long walk out to the barn. Austin talked about his concerns while they re-stacked the hay and fed the livestock. After Austin opened up to him, his grandfather put his hand on his shoulder.

"Austin, you are my oldest grand-child. You have always been special to me for I can see a lot of your dad in you. You are mature well beyond your years, but let me say this. One of the reasons your dad was such a great wartime aviator is because he flew with such abandon. He was willing to take a risk for he knew the Germans were very meticulous about the way they flew. Your dad would sometimes fly upside down as he attacked! It got to where when they saw his bright red, white, and blue wings they would break off and run for home calling him the "crazy American!"

Austin smiled at his grand-father for he had never heard that story. In fact his dad never bragged about anything from the war.

"Look, my son, I am very conservative myself, but I can say this about Beth Ann and the woman which she is, enjoy yourself with her. I do think it may be a little early to start planning a wedding, especially with so much in front of you both, but graduate, make some plans for the future. Beth Ann loves you, and I promise you she is not going anywhere."

The talk with his grand-father eased his mind. After the flight back to school, Austin took Beth Ann for a Sunday afternoon ride to around Huntsville and Rogers in northern

Arkansas. On the way back to the school he stopped on a particularly spectacular view in the mountains of farms and houses far below, and put his arms around Beth Ann and said, "I love you. I have never told anyone else. Would you at least go steady with me?"

"You are something else, Austin. We are already going steady. I love you too, and I do not ever want anyone but you."

She rode back to the campus with her head on his shoulder and a smile on her face.

The rest of the semester included long talks between Austin and Beth Ann about goals and dreams, and what they wanted in a mate. It did not take too many times for both of them to realize they were experiencing something special.

Anna found Austin one day waiting for Beth Ann to come out of class, gave him a hug and said, "You are in trouble, Austin. I know the signs, and you are in love with my roomie. However, it is extremely mutual. I cannot get her to talk about anything or anyone but you."

"Now, that is funny. My roomie said the same thing about me!"

"Ain't love grand? Well, gotta go, here comes your main squeeze."

"Such language! She is my ONLY squeeze." They smiled at one another as Beth Ann walked up to Austin and took his hand.

Chapter Nine

School was over in mid May, and Austin drove Beth Ann to her home in Alabama in his car. The servants were happy to be seeing Mister Austin again when she called to tell the staff to get the house ready.

When the few members of the Davis family came around to see what they could steal, they had had a confrontation with Samuel. For the family believed, since Mrs. Davis had passed, they were entitled to anything they wanted.

Beth Ann proved to have the mettle of her mother when it came to business. She made one phone call to the Chief of Police who was a personal friend of her and her dad. He had also seen Beth Ann on numerous occasions as she grew up, and treated her as a daughter.

He went to the man which claimed to be a distant cousin, and had collected a painting and some antiques, and explained in a very harsh tone, "Why didn't Samuel shoot you? I told him if anyone would not take no for an answer, to shoot 'em and I would rule it a justifiable homicide! Do I make myself clear?"

"Yes, sir." He hung his head in shame and he was very appreciative Beth Ann did not press charges.

"If money would do to me what I see you people do which have money, I would never want it! You never came around one time, when Mr. and Mrs. Davis were alive, to help

Beth Ann care for them while they were sick. She had put her college education on hold to come home and nurse her mother. Her mother dying in just a few days was in a way a good thing for Beth Ann. If I catch <u>anyone</u> on the property, I will arrest them! It is off limits until Beth Ann gets here in a few days. That's <u>her</u> home now!"

Samuel and the two women, Hattie and Mattie, laughed at how quick everyone quit coming around while they related the story to Beth Ann and Austin. The visit by the Police Chief made them have a new understanding.

"How long are you staying, Mister Austin?"

"At least long enough to go for another drive in the Duesenberg!" He smiled at Beth

Ann as she put her arm through his.

Later, after a huge meal of Southern cooking at its finest with fried chicken, new potatoes, turnip greens, and apple pie, all served by Hattie and Mattie. Austin and Beth Ann asked all three of the staff to sit down at the table and eat if they wished, or at least have dessert and coffee with them. The little threesome seemed nervous as if they were concerned they were being let go. Austin and Beth Ann addressed their employment concern first.

"I wanted to thank you personally for your years of service, and want to assure you that you have a job as long as you want to stay. Austin is officially my fiance, and we have talked at length about the things we would like to see changed. This is not the Old South. Hopefully we are a long way from slavery. I know what each of you make in salary, and it is not enough to educate or raise a family. These three envelopes contain a check for each of you for one thousand dollars, and beginning this moment you will make a fair salary based on what you do. You are <u>employees</u> from now on, not servants."

The three black employees did not say anything for a long minute. They looked at Beth Ann and Austin as if they had not heard correctly.

"I just don't know what to say," began Samuel, the oldest at 45 years old. "We have not had families because we lived here. Although, I <u>do</u> have a couple of kids in town by a fine woman which I go see once or twice a week." He smiled, a little bashful at the disclosure.

"We knew, Samuel. We gave her a little money along, and on birthdays and holidays, and made her promise not to tell you! You have been here ten years and we wanted to keep you."

"And here I thought she was just good at managing her money!" laughed Samuel.

"What about you girls?" asked Austin.

"Hattie is 26 and I am 28, and we have had dates, but we could not quit working to get married. We give money to our mother who is working too. We have a little brother who is 20, and we are helping him get through his last year of college at Tuskegee. We want him to make a lawyer or a doctor. We believe he will not forget who helped get him there," confessed Mattie.

By then Austin was tearing up a little. He thought about an entire family working for pocket change per day to make a difference in one family member's life, so that he could help all of them.

"We would like to meet your family, including your mother and brother, girls, and your kids and wife to be, Samuel. Are you listening?" Austin was looking straight at him, and Samuel knew he planned for him to get married.

"Have the pastor of the little church you go to perform the ceremony in front of your friends and family. We want to be invited to the wedding, fair enough?"

"Yes sir, Mister Austin, and of course, you too, Miss Beth Ann!"

The staff was invited to continue living within the Davis house, but there was a new schedule and they were each only working 6 days a week, 8 hours a day. Hattie and Mattie alternated days off, and one worked early and one evenings to continue coverage for meals and cleaning. Samuel had Wednesdays off completely. He was asked to leave a phone number or call in once or twice, if he could. Austin had his car if he and Beth Ann ever needed to go out, and the only time Samuel would ever need to work on his day off was something special. Compared to the schedule which they had worked for years, the staff felt they were being treated more than fair. For the first time the staff was invited to use the swimming pool and outdoor grilling and party facilities if they were off duty and the facilities were not being used.

It did not take but a few days for the news to spread all over town the changes at the Davis home. Jim Davis, Beth Ann's uncle had been conspicuous because he had not already been by to see Beth Ann, and he called and wanted to see her at his office. She invited him to the house, because she did not want to go into town. He was there at two o'clock that afternoon.

Beth Ann went to the door when she heard

the knock. She opened to her Uncle Jim, and he was not smiling at all.

"Are you having to answer the door yourself these days? I heard you no longer have servants, only employees."

"If you mean Hattie and Mattie, I told them I would answer the door because it was probably you. Come in. Would you like a cup of tea or coffee?"

"No, I can't stay long. I needed to ask you what you are going to do about Davis Publishing."

"Why? Is something wrong? I have never received a profit and loss statement, and I asked the accountant to give me one."

He was a little brusque as he tried to hide his surprise and said, "Why, what are you trying to find?"

"Is there something I will find?"

He flushed a little as he assured her, "No, nothing like that. I was afraid you were looking for something bad."

"Uncle Jim, I went to the bank and there is very little money in the accounts of the business or my personal account. Why is that? You told Mother we were doing well. You personally have several hundred thousand in your account."

"Oh, do you need some money, is that it?"

"The point is, I am supposed to already have money, and I don't. Against the advice of my lawyer, I am giving you 24 hours to do what you need to do to make everything right before the auditors come in. My dad and

179

mother trusted you. Are we in agreement?"

"Yes, Beth Ann. Thank you."

He treated her with respect as he shook her hand and quickly left.

The audit revealed suspected wrong doing, but several hundred thousand dollars appeared in Beth Ann's bank account and she declined to prosecute. She and Austin sat and talked about options.

"Some friends of my uncle have expressed an interest in buying the company. What do you think?"

"For <u>you</u> to run it, you would have to put your college on hold. Do you think you could trust your uncle now? If so, I think you should require consistency in profit and loss statements, and reports to find any irregularities before they happen. I know I am selfish, but I want you to come back to school with me. You can sell later once you decide what you want."

Beth Ann smiled at him, put her arms around his waist, and said, "What if I decide I want you?"

"That is a distinct possibility. I can not imagine my future without you in it, Beth Ann."

There was a meeting with Uncle Jim, Beth Ann's lawyer, and the accounting firm she had hired. Austin was present, but Jim quietly and privately asked Beth Ann, "You are a very rich young lady, Beth Ann. You could probably cash out for over a million dollars. Do you think there is a possibility this guy from

Arkansas is after you for your money?"

Beth laughed at him, "You are a fool, Uncle Jim. Austin Johnson himself is a multi-millionaire, and his family is worth over a hundred million. No, his family might be asking am I after <u>his</u> money!"

Jim Davis was stunned. The thought of that much money made him start smiling at Austin, for surely once Beth Ann and he were married there would be a way to get some of it.

"Will you be okay for a few minutes? I need to take Samuel and go into town." asked Austin the next morning.

"Sure. Hattie and Mattie are helping me change the furniture around."

With a kiss and a, "See you later," Austin

and Samuel drove into Birmingham and went to a jewelry store Austin saw while driving around in downtown. He went in and asked to see engagement and wedding rings. Samuel smiled and promised to not tell anyone.

After the evening meal, Austin and Beth Ann were sitting out by the pool under an umbrella. The scent of magnolias permeated the air so heavy it seemed to be the air itself.

"We really have not decided where we go from here, have we, Beth Ann?"

"I don't know. Do you have any thoughts?"

"Yeah, I do. Let me have your glass. I will go freshen our drinks. I don't know where everybody is."

Over her shoulder he could see three sets of eyes peering around the curtains. He went inside and put more ice in their glasses, and poured the tea. He pulled a little black box from his pocket, put it on the tray, and winked at the threesome who all were smiling at him.

"Here you go. Have I told you lately I love you? I probably haven't since this morning, but I do."

Beth Ann took her glass of tea from the tray and looked at the small black box.

"What is that?"

"Well, I'll be. Open it for I am curious too."

Beth figured Austin had purchased the new ear rings which they had seen at the jewelry store. She opened it to see a huge diamond engagement ring. She looked at Austin who was smiling but had tears in his eyes.

"Beth Ann Davis, will you marry me?"

Austin was still standing, but Beth Ann stood, grabbed him and hugged him and shouted, "Yes, yes, yes!" The motion almost put them backwards into the pool.

From the doorway came Samuel, Hattie, and Mattie. All were in tears but were clapping as they gathered around the couple.

"Miss Beth Ann, we know you two are going to be happy together. I am so proud for you both!" exclaimed Samuel.

They gathered around Austin and Beth Ann, and Hattie and Mattie had already baked a cake.

"How did you know I was going to say yes?"

"If you hadn't, I would have run off with him myself!" laughed Hattie.

Beth Ann hugged the girls and Samuel. "Thank you. You are all the family I have and I am glad you are here to share it with me."

Beth Ann pointed her finger at Austin and said, "You are a little scamp! I had no idea!"

"Well, Samuel and I went to town to buy some things for the lawn, and I thought to myself, I wonder if Beth Ann would like to get married?" Austin laughed, and Beth Ann just shook her head.

"I think we could get married right here, don't you? My dad and uncle can fly everyone into Birmingham. I just want my family around, not a bunch of strangers. Plus, if we have it here, our staff can attend. No one makes a better cake than Hattie and Mattie."

"What about your folks?"

"Pack a few clothes and we will drive over and spring the surprise on them. If we leave around 5 in the morning, we can eat supper in Little Rock. Yall start making plans for a wedding!" Austin told the jubilant threesome.

Around 5 o'clock in the afternoon the next day, James, Payton, Anna, and Fred were sitting by the pool and visiting about Beth Ann and Austin. Anna thought Austin would like to marry her roomie, but he was so secretive about everything to do with his life she told them they would have to read about it in the paper.

They were still laughing as a car drove into the driveway, came around the corner of the house to the garage which was close to the pool. They heard, "Beep, beep, beep!" It was

Austin's signature "horn hello!"

Austin was just opening the door for Beth Ann when the group from the pool plus Austin and Anna's parents came running up to them.

With a big grin like he had been up to something mischievous, Austin stood with his arm around Beth Ann and said, "Folks, if you have not met her, I would like to introduce you to my fiancee, Beth Ann Davis!"

Anna started jumping up and down and hugging Beth Ann, while Fred and James were pumping August's hand as if they were trying to prime a well. Luke and Maddie hugged Beth Ann, and Maddie exclaimed, "Finally, I get a daughter-in-law! You are so welcome into this family!"

Levi and Ellen of course remembered

meeting Beth Ann when they flew over to Birmingham for her mother's funeral. They still embraced, and told her how glad they were for both of them. As they walked into the house, Anna walked between Austin and Beth Ann with her arms around both of them.

"Who would ever have guessed this would happen the day we met, roomie? Certainly not your mother!"

They smiled at one another, and Beth Ann said, "Believe it or not, Mother picked Austin for the man she wanted me to marry, and she loved you as my friend. She told me she could pass and not worry about me, because you two would take care of me. Truthfully, it may be why she did not fight too hard to stay alive."

Anna hugged her hard and said, "We will."

189

After a meal of sandwiches and salads fixed by John and Lydia, who were also proud to see the way things turned out, the group sat and talked about which date to have the wedding. When told Austin and Beth Ann were considering having the wedding in Birmingham, Luke said, "Look, let us fly over and pick up the staff and whoever else wants to come, and have it at the Country Club here in Little Rock."

Austin and Beth Ann looked at one another and Beth Ann shrugged her shoulders and smiled, "Sure. Why not?"

It was already the first week of June and it was decided to have the wedding at 10 o'clock in the morning on June 29th, which was the last Saturday of the month, because Beth Ann wanted to be a June bride. Plus, having it early in the day would help get away from the heat.

Maddie, Ellen, and Anna took Beth Ann the next day and bought her a wedding dress after trying on most of the dresses in Little Rock. With her mother gone, the Johnson women decided they wanted to buy the bride a dress.

James was to be the Best Man, and Fred and Anna were in the wedding, of course, with Anna as Maid of Honor. The wedding was to be at the Country Club with August Johnson doing the honors.

Austin had several talks with his mother and dad and told them he was thinking about transferring to the University of Alabama in Tuscaloosa.

"Oh, my prodigal son! Don't break your daddy's heart!" Luke did smile, however, and ask why.

"Here is my logic. We already live on the southwestern side of Birmingham and we could commute from our home to school. We will hopefully be able to not have classes every day of the week, and not have to drive the 50 or 60 miles round trip to school but a maximum of three days a week. If not, another scenario is to rent an apartment closer to school and come home a couple times a week. Don't look so serious, you guys. Alabama even has a football team! I have already talked to the Alabama coaching legend, Frank Thomas, and he said he would be glad to have me. Last season they only lost to Tennessee and

Mississippi State. This year they are hoping for a national ranking. With my help they might!" Luke grinned.

"You mean to tell me my son is going to play for another team? You would lift your hands against your brothers? What is this world coming to?"

Luke laughed, but he put his his hands on his shoulders and smiled at him. "Your plan to move and live in Alabama makes perfect sense to me, Austin. Beth Ann needs to keep her house and business going. She has a great staff to help her, and with you by her side I expect to hear great things from you two."

"You forgive your prodigal son then?"

"Yes, and so did the father in the Bible, but I know a little now how he felt." Everyone laughed at the remark.

A week before the wedding, Levi and Luke went over in their plane and picked up Mattie, Hattie and Samuel. The girls' mother and Samuel's new bride also came.

John and Lydia were disappointed at first to not be doing the cake, but after Austin put his arm around them and explained the staff from Birmingham wanted to have a part, they were appreciative of the extra help.

John told Austin how much he understood longtime loyalty. He shook Austin's hand because he had already heard of the emancipation of the staff and their promotion from servants to staff. He bowed to Austin and said, "I am proud of you. I taught you well." Austin hugged him and said, "Yes, you did, old friend. Yes, you did."

After a beautiful wedding at the Country Club, Austin borrowed his dad's plane and flew to Richard Allen's estate in Palm Springs, California. For over a week the newlyweds were taken to Hollywood and toured Los Angeles and the surrounding beaches. Through Richard's connections as a movie producer, they met several movie stars and celebrities. It was a "dream" honeymoon.

Austin and Beth Ann flew back to Little Rock for a few days, and then drove their car back to Birmingham. The staff was glad to see the new couple and clapped as Austin carried Beth Ann over the threshold into the house.

"I am so glad to be back home."

"Anywhere you are is home, Beth Ann."

Austin began a routine of getting up early and working out and running to get ready for football. Beth Ann played tennis and went swimming with him, and at times jogged along with him for shorter distances. By the middle of August and the start of "two a days'" Austin was a lean, tan, muscular, six feet two and 205 pounds.

The Alabama football team was coming off a good 1940 season with only two losses, Tennessee and Mississippi State. It was Alabama's third loss in a row to the University of Tennessee. The team went 7-2 overall and 4-2 in the Southeastern Conference. Acquiring Austin Johnson to be used on defense as well as wide receiver completed the team as far as

Frank Thomas was concerned.

The 1941 season was an interesting one. Alabama beat Tulane 19-14 in spite of being outplayed in yardage. Special team play and Austin returning a punt for a touchdown was the key to victory. Their record was 9-2 overall and 5-2 in conference play. It was successful enough to be invited to play Texas A&M in the Cotton Bowl.

Texas A&M outgained the Tide 309 yards to 75. Alabama made one first down and A&M made 13. However, unbelievably, Texas A&M had 12 turnovers, including seven inter- ceptions and five fumbles. Alabama scored on a punt return and an interception return. Texas A&M fumbled on their 21 and 24 yard line twice and Alabama scored on both possessions. They also kicked a field goal after an A&M fumble on the 17 yard line.

A few days later, on their way home from church on the first Sunday in December, people were running around in the street and yelling, "The war has started! The Japs bombed Pearl Harbor!"

All evening and into the night people were sitting by their radios listening to the results of the sneak attack. The next day President Roosevelt declared war on the Japanese. Austin called home to talk to his dad.

"What should I do, Dad? With war declared, should I enlist?"

"James has already called too, but I think both of you need to stay in school for now. Like the First World War, good leaders which both of you will make with a college education, will be in demand. This will be another long and bloody war, my sons. Trust me, you will have a chance to fight."

Austin called James and invited him to Birmingham for a few days after school was out in May 1942. He drove over in his 1936 Ford Convertible. Although Beth Ann set him up with a date or two with pretty girls which she knew, he explained he and Payton were close to getting engaged. The only thing keeping it from happening was the war and school. He and Payton were just Sophomores at the University of Arkansas, and neither was ready for marriage, even though they were going steady and had been together for over two years.

In addition to home dates in Legion Field in Birmingham and Denny Stadium on campus in Tuscaloosa, the Tide played one game each at Cramton Bowl in Montgomery and Ladd Stadium in Mobile during the 1942 season.

A safety on a fumbled kickoff and a 38-yard touchdown run by running back Tom Jenkins were enough for an 8-0 win over Tennessee. However, in a game that decided the SEC championship for 1942, Alabama blew a 10-0 fourth quarter lead against Georgia. Frank Sinkwich, who went on to win the Heisman Trophy for 1942, threw two touchdown passes in the fourth, followed by a fumble return for a TD which iced Georgia's 21-10 victory.

With the United States mobilizing for World War II and millions of men joining the armed forces, Alabama's schedule for 1942 included two games against military all-star teams. 'Bama won 27-0 against Pensacola Naval Air Station, a team that included former Alabama end Ben McLeod as well as players formerly of Fordham, LSU and Nebraska, but lost to a Georgia Pre-Flight squad that boasted former All-Americans from Tennessee and Tulane as well as other players with college experience.

Alabama's first ever Orange Bowl was a wild affair against Boston College. Alabama trailed 14-0 at the end of the first quarter, scored 22 points in the second quarter to go into halftime up 22-21, then dominated the second half to win the game 37-21. [1]

Christmas of 1942 was spent in Little Rock. With nice-sized bonuses for the staff, Austin and Beth Ann closed up the house and traveled over from Birmingham. James and Anna came home from the university, and it was a joyous occasion. Two days before Christmas, after another huge John and Lydia meal, everyone was sitting around the fire in the family room. James put a log on the fire, turned and looked at the room and his father.

"Things are in chaos in the world, Dad. I have a friend on Guadalcanal. I haven't heard from him or about him. So, I guess he is okay."

"Are you feeling guilty about not already volunteering?"

"Maybe a little. I will at least finish the school year, but I may enlist in the Army Air

202

Corps. I want to be a fighter pilot. I already have a pilot's license. I have been told I could go."

"What about you, Austin?" asked Luke.

"I hate to say it, but James is right. There is already talk Alabama is not going to field a football team for the 1943 season. I want to fly also. I have been watching the progress of the new P-51 Mustang and I want to fly it. That is one sweet airplane."

"Okay, what about you, Anna?" asked Levi.

I have been talking to the people about becoming a WASP and ferrying planes from the United States to Europe. They would not let me be a fighter pilot."

"I have to tell you, kids, it breaks my heart

203

to think of you in harm's way, but Levi and I went too. So, I am not going to even try to talk you out of it. I just will be praying for you every moment of every day."

"What about me?" spoke up Beth Ann. "I may not be a combatant, but what I do is needed also. My publishing company received a contract from the War Department to print materials for everything from posters and propaganda to training manuals."

Austin put his arm around her and said softly, "Everyone is going to be just as proud of you as if you were a combatant. The war will have to be a team effort to win on so many fronts against so many countries. This is definitely a World War!" He kissed her on the cheek and held her tight for a moment.

The little group was quiet for a moment, and Luke said, "Let us pray."

Back home in Alabama, Austin and Beth Ann began to produce propaganda and training manuals while continuing to attend school. Beth Ann was impressed with how articulate Austin could be. He did most of the writing and she had to do very little editing to send it to the printers. The Navy Handbook required numerous pictures, and Austin took most of them using a press camera given to him by his Uncle Levi. It was left over from the days when he was a reporter for the Arkansas Gazette. After seeing some of his work, he told Austin he would give him a job, and Austin actually entertained the idea of being a War correspondent, but he wanted to fly.

In July 1943 Austin and James applied for Army flight school. After a 60 day officer candidate boot camp in Alabama they went home for 10 days. Austin went to Alabama and James stayed in Little Rock. Both were Lieutenant Junior Grade after having two to three years of college and graduating from OCS.

Austin and Beth Ann spent every moment together at their home in Alabama, but James and Payton at home in Little Rock felt they wanted to wait about getting married. In late October they both received orders to Lubbock, Texas, for flight training at the Lubbock Army Airfield.

Lubbock, Texas, in 1943 had a population of approximately 30,000 which grew quickly during and after the war. The city had given 2000 acres a few years before to build an Army Training facility, and in the years from 1938 to 1943 Lubbock had trained several thousand aviators. The training field was deemed safer than most by being surrounded with miles of flat farmland and blessed with a usually sunny, though sometimes cold in the winter, weather most of the year. It receives on the average of less than 19 inches of rain per year.

"Is this it?" grumbled James. "The only green I see around here is uniforms."

"Welcome to West Texas in the wintertime," smiled the non-com there to pick them up who had heard the remark. "Don't worry, you will grow to love it."

"Yeah, I am sure I will," frowned James. He

and Austin loaded their duffel bags into the Jeep and turned their collars up to the wind.

The ride in the jeep with no heater, and the top letting in the air with no windows, was bone chilling and numbing. Luckily the train ran close to the main gate. The driver stopped at the gate as Austin and James presented documents which allowed them on the base. The driver was friendly and even helped unload their bags in front of the barracks. He showed them where to find bunks and linens, and where the chow hall was.

"Thanks, man. I guess we are all set. We owe you one."

"Sounds good to me. You can buy a round at Pinky's. Oh, Pinky's is a local bar where mostly local veterans and soldiers hang out when we are not in class."

They both smiled and Austin said, "Will do! But it has to be warm. I am numb from the cold!"

The non-com smiled back and said, "Know what you mean. I am from Arizona. You never get used to this place!"

They found the non-com's name was Thomas Scott, and everyone called him Scottie. He was as laid back as James and he was well liked. It was worth a drink just to get to hang out with him he was so much fun. He was only 5 foot 5, black hair and blue eyes. The girls stood in line to dance with him.

Austin called home collect just to make sure Beth Ann was able to take care of business without him. They visited for only about 10 minutes, and Beth Ann said, "Austin, don't worry about me. You keep focused on what you are doing. I am fine. Samuel and the girls are taking good care of me and send their love."

"I know, but I miss you. I love you."

"I love you too. Say hello to James for me."

"I will. I will call at least once a week. Goodbye, my love."

The first Saturday night on the base Scottie came by the barracks and told Austin, "I see you and James checked out a Jeep. I am going on in to Pinky's with a couple of the guys, and do a little "trolling" before the crowd comes. I'll see you guys there." He smiled and winked and Austin just shook his head.

About an hour later, after standing in line to check out the Jeep, Austin and James took two more soldiers with them and drove into Lubbock, commented on the rough red brick streets of downtown, and out to "the Strip."

The Lubbock city fathers did not allow the purchase of liquor inside the city limits, and the bars and package stores were relegated to a stretch of the Andrews highway south of town nicknamed "the Strip." To Austin and James it was somewhat hypocritical in that the bars were usually full of locals.

As the jeep pulled into the parking lot, they saw a crowd of people watching a fight with 3 locals and one hapless soldier in a bloody uniform. One burly cowboy was raising his arm back to hit the soldier held up by two more laughing drunk cowboys when it was gripped in a painful vise that pushed him down to his knees.

"That's enough," said Austin through gritted teeth. "The fight is over. Unless you want to continue it with me!"

The cowboy rubbed on his forearm which bore the hand print of Austin's grip. He gazed up at Austin and said, "That's quite a grip you got there, soldier boy."

The obvious pain showed as he stood up. His friends let go of the soldier and James caught the semi-conscious young man in his arms.

"Why, it is Scottie!" he exclaimed.

Austin turned and glared at the big cowboy.

"He was trying to pick up my girl. He was already dancing his second dance with her."

"Sounds like he had already picked her up. She probably was tired of an asinine buffoon like you pawing and slobbering at her. She wanted a gentleman."

There were several mutterings and laughs from the crowd who were afraid of Dixon and his rough friends.

"I have heard about men like you, Dixon. You are a coward, and too afraid to go fight for your country, but to feel like a man you beat up young soldiers. Well, that stops tonight."

"You know, soldier boy. The numbers are not very good for you. There are three of us and only two of you," smirked Dixon.

"You know, you are right. We need to even

it up a little." Austin looked at a red-headed drunk cowboy who was urging on Dixon. Austin pointed a finger at him and said evenly, "What about you, carrot top? Why don't you help Dixon and these other low lifes out so the fight will be fair? After my brother and I kick your butts all over this parking lot, I don't want anyone to be able to say it wasn't a fair fight, okay?"

As the cowboy's face turned red, he started to take a step toward the two brothers, Dixon put out a hand and stopped him.

"No, he's mine. I am gonna carve him like a turkey," he scowled. He pulled an 8 inch bladed hunting knife from a sheath on his belt. He held it out in front of him.

Austin smiled at him, and said, "Hey,

Dixon, watch this!" In one quick move, Austin kicked the man's hand and caused the knife to fly into the air. As Dixon looked up in astonishment, he did not see Austin's kick coming hard enough to crush his chest and send him backwards into the arms of his companions. They held Dixon up as the knife came down into Austin's waiting hand.

The two men's eyes opened wide as Austin jumped nimbly into the air and kicked both men in the face as they held on to Dixon. The Washu move caught both men by surprise as they fell back on the ground letting Dixon fall. Their noses were both broken and one had lost two front teeth as they lay on the ground groaning and looking at their blood dripping on the gravel parking lot.

"Okay, carrot top your turn. It is just you and me!"

The man cursed and said, "No sir! I have seen enough. If you will let me go, I promise I will never pick a fight with a soldier again!"

The crowd roared at the remark and carrot top's hasty departure.

Dixon was having trouble breathing from his broken sternum, and he put his hand up and cringed as Austin stood over him and pulled him up by the front of his shirt with his left hand with the knife still in his right.

"Don't cut me! You win! I'm through!" He could barely talk, but his eyes were showing his fear.

"One last thing. I ever hear of you doing anything but buying a soldier a drink I will come for you and your friends. Next time I won't play fair. Do I make myself clear?"

Dixon was very polite as he wheezed , "Yes sir!"

"Now pick up your friends and go. I don't want to even see you for a long time.!"

Dixon grimaced at the pain in his chest as he and his friends limped to their pickup while the crowd jeered and laughed.

As Austin and James turned to look for Scottie, they discovered the pretty blonde cowgirl Dixon was trying to say was his girlfriend had Scottie's head cradled in her lap and was tenderly washing his mostly superficial wounds.

"Oh brother," laughed James as he rolled his eyes at the scene. Scottie opened his eyes,

217

smiled, winked, and pulled the girl's hand back to his face and groaned a not very convincing sound. She went back to rubbing his forehead as he had his eyes closed and a smile on his face.

"Do you think he will survive the terrible beating he took from Dixon?" Austin asked with a big grin.

"He may not make it back to the base tonight, but, oh yeah, he is in fine hands!"

They both laughed and entered the bar which erupted in a standing ovation. Even the locals had been afraid of Dixon and his cronies, but now it would take some time for their wounds to heal before they confronted anyone else. Both brothers ordered their first beers and both agreed they could not understand why anyone would like that bitter taste. After forcing down two though, the room began to spin, and they knew it was time to go. They drove back to the base where the officer at the gate saluted and said, "Thanks for taking care of a problem for our men. He had beat up so many guys we were told to go to Pinky's at our own risk. Glad to have you aboard!"

Austin returned the man's salute and he and James went to the barracks. They undressed down to uniform pants and undershirts and socks. Both lay down to rest, and with everyone else in town on a Saturday night, they started talking to one another.

"Let's drive into town and go to church tomorrow," said Austin.

"I guess we probably need to after tonight,"

219

answered James. They both smiled.

The next day they went to the big First Baptist Church on Broadway close to Texas Tech. Both men enjoyed the service, and there were numerous service personnel and their families from the base.

On the way back to the base, James told Austin, "You're fun, Austin, but I miss going to church with Payton and Mom and Dad."

"We are going to be okay, James. At least we have one another, and we know everyone at home are praying for us every day. Let's go find something to eat!"

Chapter Ten

After a week of hanging around the base and watching the bulletin boards of when they were going to start their training, finally Austin and James were called into the base commander's office.

Sitting at a long table with stacks of papers in front of them, were three officers which the only one the two recognized was the base commander.

"I see on your application to flight school you both already know how to fly a little," the base commander spoke first.

Standing at attention, Austin spoke first,

"Sir, we both have had our pilots' licenses since we were 16 years old. We learned to fly single and multi-engine aircraft from being taught to fly the family's twin engine Beechcraft and the single engine Curtiss JN-4. We both have logged over 2400 hours in different aircraft including the JN-4 we were taught on, and I personally own a Piper Cub I am just finishing restoring."

"Well, well, well, Mr. Austin Johnson and Mr. James Johnson, that is interesting news indeed." The base commander looked at the other two officers and nodded as he smiled.

"Your country needs good pilots, but we also need men to train those good pilots. After your initial 7 month flight training, we will have two training billets here in Lubbock open if you would be interested. We don't need an answer this minute, but be thinking along those lines as you move through training.

Austin, I see here you are married. If you become a training officer, your wife could join you in on base housing. It might not be too bad in West Texas if you had your wife here. Besides, it might keep you out of trouble. I heard about the liaison work you two performed in neutralizing a local group of ruffians a couple of weeks ago. Unofficially, well done, but also let's remember why we are here, and keep the "making friends" to a minimum." He smiled, and when he did, the others followed suit. Austin and James snapped their heels together, saluted, and the base commander said, "Dismissed!"

The next morning was a clear, cold, West Texas day with little wind. In the cockpit of the AT-6 Texan used for training, Austin listened to the flight instructor run through the preflight check as did James in his airplane. Both were going on their first orientation flights. Both had already walked around the planes checking the tires, free movement of the control surfaces, such as the rudder and ailerons. When the instructors were satisfied with the physical condition of the exteriors, they started the engines and began to let them warm up to operating temperature.

After the little JN-4's which Austin and James had been flying, the AT-6 Texan aircraft seemed to be a very advanced airplane. As the instructor opened the throttle, the plane rose from the runway very easily into the air.

They only flew over and around the base at first, and then climbed to an altitude of approximately 3000 feet. The instructors kept up a running conversation through the headsets as they pointed out local landmarks, neighboring towns, and navigation coordinates to familiarize the two with Lubbock and Lubbock County from the air.

After flying for about 30 minutes, Austin's flight instructor, Bill Burnett, asked Austin, "What do you think? Think you can learn to fly one of these?"

"Of course. Let me try it for a few minutes."

The instructor had seen several air cadets come through the training course which could fly a little, but he was not prepared for a student which could fly as well, or maybe even better, than he could!

"I am impressed. Who taught you to fly?"

"My dad and uncle, who are twin brothers, were fighter pilots and flight instructors during World War I, and they have had James and me and our first cousin, Anna Lee, as co-pilots ever since we could sit up or walk. I had a solo flight before I was 12 years old, and my dad let James and me fly on every flight to and from all sorts of destinations. They have business interests in California, and even delivered the mail at one point, although the company sold out later."

"What happened to your cousin?"

"She is training to become a WASP and ferry bombers across to Europe. She's a pistol!

If any woman can take care of herself, she can!" Austin laughed. He then surprised Bill by doing a surprise barrel roll.

"This little trainer is really fun to fly, isn't it?"

Bill grinned into his face mask, "Yes, it is! But you don't want the Old Man to know I let a new cadet do a barrel roll on his first flight!"

"I sure won't tell him, but it felt so willing I was never uncomfortable at any time, were you?"

"Nope, not a bit. I knew I could trust your flying. Let's head for home. It's a tradition the cadet buys the trainer the first round after their orientation flight."

"You're lying. I will have to remember that line when I train my own cadets." Austin laughed out loud. "But I will be glad to buy!"

The North American T-6 Texan was known as the "pilot maker" because of its important role in preparing pilots for combat. Derived from the 1935 North American NA-16 prototype, a cantilever, low wing monoplane, the Texan filled the need for a basic combat trainer during World War II and beyond.

North American's rapid production of the T-6 Texan coincided with the wartime expansion of the United States air war commitment. As of 1940, the required flight hours for combat pilots to earn their wings had been cut to only 200 during a much shortened training period of seven months. Of those hours, 75 were logged in the AT-6.

It had a maximum speed of 205 mph and a ceiling of 21,500 feet making it a forgiving, durable trainer.

Austin was even allowed to land the plane. It was a very soft landing and afterward Bill was complimented by the tower captain how well he landed. He looked at Austin as they carried their flight gear into the locker room, smiled, and winked.

Later that evening the foursome of Austin, James, Bill Burnett, and Dennis Duryea, Austin's trainer, were sitting in a nearly empty Pinky's Bar and Grill. They all got a laugh when Bill told the story how surprised the tower captain would have been to know it was Austin which had landed the plane, not him. Austin and James purchased a pitcher of draft beer apiece and the conversation finally took a more serious note.

Bill asked, "Have you and James thought any more about becoming flight instructors?"

"We have talked a little. How long have you been here?" asked Austin.

"I have been here 18 months. I love having my family here, but I am itching to leave and feeling a little guilty about not fighting alongside my students. I am one of the billets which, if you take the instructor position, will be replaced."

"How does your wife feel?" James asked.

"She's a good Army wife, and she knows how I feel. She and my son will move back to Russellville, Arkansas, to live in our home we left. You probably don't even know where that is."

"Sure we do. My dad and uncle grew up in Paris right up the road from Russellville. My grandfather is a Pentecostal preacher in Paris still today!"

"I thought you were from Alabama."

"I am from Little Rock, and met and married a pretty young thing named Beth Ann Davis from Birmingham, Alabama, which I met at the University of Arkansas. She has a business there and we moved to Birmingham to let her run it after her folks passed away. I transferred to the University of Alabama for two years before I joined the Army."

"Are you the same notorious Austin Johnson which played football for the University of Alabama just a couple of years

231

ago?"

"Yep," smiled Austin.

"I happened to read about you returning that punt which won the game when you guys beat Tulane. Also, the bowl game against Texas A&M was on the radio. You were a standout there too! You had three interceptions!"

The only patrons in the bar were a couple of middle-aged people and a large table of Texas Tech students who had heard the conversation about Austin. One of the students came over and spoke to Austin.

"I am not trying to intrude at all, Mister Johnson, but I don't guess you would want to play for Tech, would you?" said a smiling, slender, dark haired young man wearing glasses and a sport coat and tie. He had two

232

giggling blonde girlfriends standing with him which kept batting their eyes at the four young soldiers.

"Thank you for the compliment, but no, my football is put on hold until after my enlistment."

"Fair enough. We are glad to have you in Lubbock, and if you have a chance, the basketball team is starting to play conference games soon if you wanted to come and watch them play."

"You know what? I would like that. Thank you for the invitation." He held out his hand and the young man shook his hand. The two girls and the rest of the table gathered around and shook hands, and one or two of the girls even hugged the soldiers. The men ate,

233

finished their drinks, and left for the base smiling and waving at the students.

As Austin and James walked into the barracks, there was a note laying on Austin's bunk to call Anna at a phone number he did not recognize. He called the number and a female voice answered, "Women Airforce Service Pilots, to whom did you wish to speak?"

"This is Austin Johnson, and I am a family member of Anna Johnson. I missed her call and I am returning it. Is she around there close?"

"Yes she is. Hold on I can see her!" The girl held the phone and yelled, "Anna some guy is calling and says he is a family member!"

A breathless Anna picked up the phone and said excitedly into the phone as to who it could be, "Hello?"

"Hey troublemaker, are you still raising a ruckus? Where are you?"

"Austin! You won't believe this! I am in Sweetwater, Texas, for WASP training just an hour away by air! How's James?"

"He's fine and here with me. We took our first orientation flights today. We are training in the AT-6 and it is a neat little plane. I even did a barrel roll and secretly landed it on my first flight!"

"You didn't! They are so protective with us women it is boring. I have been meaning to call but I have only been here a couple of weeks and this is my first chance."

She got to visit for a few minutes with James and they all agreed the first time possible they were going to get together.

Both air training facilities were shutting down for Thanksgiving weekend in two weeks and Anna had talked her dad into flying the family to Lubbock after picking her up, and they would spend the weekend together in Lubbock.

Chapter Eleven

On August 5, 1943, the Women's Flying Training Detachment (WFTD) and the Women's Auxiliary Ferrying Squadron (WAFS) were combined to form the paramilitary WASP (Women Airforce Service Pilots) organization.

Twenty-five thousand women applied to join the Wasp, but only 1,830 were accepted and took the oath, and out of those only 1,074 women passed the training and joined, becoming the first women to fly American military aircraft.

After Austin and James left for Lubbock at the end of October 1943, Anna Lee joined the WASP. One of the requirement's for all WASP was to have a pilot's license, and she had hers from the time she was 16 years old. Fred and she were engaged unofficially but he hurt his knee in training after joining the Army, and was transferring to Washington to accept an attache position with Colonel Talbert, the father of George Talbert, his friend and teammate at the University of Arkansas.

The thought of being alone in Little Rock was a big reason she was ready to leave. Anna and Fred had talked before he left for the Army and he was encouraging her to join to get her to be able to possibly fly into Washington. She had arrived in Sweetwater, Texas, in late

October, and was already flying training flights before she had the chance to call Austin and James.

Austin and James drove over to the Lubbock Municipal Airport on Wednesday afternoon before Thanksgiving Day to wait for the plane.

"Hey, there it is!" exclaimed James.

The stainless hulled Beechcraft gleamed in the late sunlight as it circled once and then settled onto the runway nice and easy.

"Must have been Dad flying," said Austin.

"Well, it probably wasn't Anna!" smiled James.

They were smiling as the plane taxied to a stop and both looked at one another as Anna waved from the cockpit.

"I can't believe it!" laughed Luke.

The door opened and the steps extended and Austin was the first to the bottom of the steps. To his surprise Beth Ann was the first one out the door and down the steps. She leaped the final two and Austin caught her in his arms and held her off the ground as he kissed her.

"What are you doing here? You did not say a word about coming!"

"The whole family cooked this up. We thought you guys might need a lift! We even have a surprise for James. Look!"

Payton was at the top of the steps, but James did not wait. He bounded up the steps and kissed her, and walked with his arm around her as they came down.

There were tears and hugs and kisses everywhere as Luke, Maddie, Levi, and Ellen came down the steps. Finally, Anna came down after shutting down the cockpit.

"You know, Anna, you are getting better at landing. James and I were worried the Army would make you pay for all the crashed aircraft!" He hugged her close with tears in his eyes. Without saying so, she knew how much the three of them cared for one another.

"We had to have three Jeeps to get everyone picked up, and I got a guy to help us by driving one of the Jeeps. There he is now."

Everyone turned to see a uniformed soldier coming out of the terminal. No one said anything for a moment, and them Anna almost screamed.

"Fred!"

She ran across the pavement and into his arms as he whirled her around and kissed her. She furrowed her brow as she asked, "But how?"

"Ask Austin. He made a call to George Talbert, who asked his dad, the colonel, and officially there happened to be a meeting come up in Lubbock. So, here I am!"

Anna turned to Austin and grabbed him and kissed him on the cheek. "I love you!" Everyone laughed.

"I will have to go by and give the base commander some papers from my dad for this to be a legitimate meeting." He smiled.

Later that evening, the little group sat in the

lobby of the Lubbock Hotel and talked about the future. Fred had asked Anna to marry him and come back to Washington D.C. with him.

"Fred, you know the answer is yes, but I am still in training in Sweetwater, and I feel very strongly about serving in the WASP. I know your mother and dad are not here, but what if we got married this weekend, go back to work, and I will see if I can get stationed in D.C. We will be deployed in over 120 different airfields, and several are around Washington. I am sure with your dad's help, okay, maybe Austin too, I can be stationed with you." She smiled: for once a little bashful at the thought of spending the night with Fred.

Anna turned to her mother and Aunt Maddie and said, "Before you get too sad. Let me say this is not a spur of the moment thing. I promise as soon as the war is over, Fred and I will renew our vows and give you the pleasure of a church wedding. Fair enough?"

Anna's mother, Ellen, said with tears in her eyes, "The ceremony is not what marriage is all about. I would not mind at all for you two to have this weekend together. I know firsthand the uncertainty of war."

The day after Thanksgiving Day, Fred and Anna were married in front of Reverend Rogers of a little Pentecostal church in Lubbock. Both were in uniform as were Austin, his best man, and James as a male attendant. Beth Ann was Maid of Honor and carried the flowers for her while Payton was bridesmaid.

Back at the hotel, Anna and Fred received

an upgrade to the bridal suite complete with a bottle of champagne which never was opened. It was cold outside on Saturday and it was about noon before the newlyweds made their appearance in the dining room. Both were embarrassed from the applause of everyone, even the patrons at the hotel when Austin stood and applauded.

Austin and James shook hands with Fred and hugged Anna.

"To think it all started with a dip in the pool!" smiled Austin at Anna.

Fred's return plane did not leave until Monday morning, but Anna had to be back before 10 p.m. Sunday night.

"It is just like being in college all over again," grumbled Anna. "Except here the house mother is a gripy old man." Then she giggled as she told the story of Austin flirting with the house mother at the University of Arkansas.

Anna and Fred were both trying to be brave for the other, but as soon as Anna was on the plane, she cried.

James and Payton decided to get married over the Christmas break and she would move to Lubbock to be near Austin and Beth Ann. The base commander was excited to have Austin and James commit to a year as training instructors after they received their wings in June 1944.

Austin and James both got a ten day leave for Christmas, and Luke flew the plane up to take everyone back to Little Rock for the wedding of Payton and James. Grandpa August agreed to perform the ceremony, and Austin was best man. Mallory, Payton's twin sister, was the Maid of Honor which meant Austin was to be her escort.

"Well hello, Austin." Mallory came up alongside and casually put her hand on Austin's back. Austin turned and one of the first things he noticed was the big diamond engagement ring on her left hand. He was relieved a little because he believed things would not get out of hand if she was already engaged.

"Well hello yourself, Miss Mallory." He smiled at her and said, "Who is the lucky guy?"

"Benny Winston has had a crush on me since we were in grade school. He begged me until I gave in!" She giggled, and just for a moment he remembered just how beautiful she was. Then he felt Beth Ann's arm snake through his and Beth Ann's silky voice.

"Why, this must be Mallory, Payton's sister. My name is Beth Ann, Austin's wife, and I am glad to meet any of Austin's friends."

To the casual <u>male</u> observer, it was just a conversation between two women who had just met. The tone of voice, the direct eye contact, her arm through Austin's, and her controlled smile, let Mallory know who she was dealing with. Beth Ann Johnson was a woman with a lifetime of dealing with little girls like Mallory, and she could more than hold her own as the wife of the best looking guy at the wedding. As a woman, the fact was not lost on Mallory, and she cleared her throat and said, "I better go find Benny. He's probably nursing a drink somewhere." She kept looking at Beth Ann but was pointing over her shoulder and waving at something vague.

"It was really nice to meet you, Mallory," purred Beth Ann as Mallory backed away. She squeezed Austin's arm to reassure him she had the situation well under control.

"Oooo. I could see the claws come out. Baby, you were something else! I imagine she will barely walk down the aisle beside me now. I have to admit, I have never been as intimidated by any man as I would have been by you if I had been a woman!"

Austin saw Mallory later at the rehearsal but she would not even make eye contact. When it came time to link arms to walk the aisle she kept her body well away from his. Beth Ann's point was well made with Mallory.

The savagery of women was not lost on Austin, and he just smiled to himself for he was very proud of Beth Ann.

After Austin, Beth Ann, James, and Payton returned to Lubbock after Christmas, the girls worked on decorating their little homes. Base housing was basic with gas stove, refrigerator, furniture including bed, chest of drawers, and living room furniture which included chair, couch and coffee table. The girls went shopping nearly every day to find prints for the walls, rugs, nicer dishes, and curtains for the windows. They repainted with different colors inside and out, and within a few days they were settled into their own first homes.

"Every day I come home it is to a different home!" exclaimed Austin.

"Are you saying you don't like it?"

"No, darling, I was just making a comment. I actually enjoy it because I know you and Payton have to be bored."

"I have been thinking that, if you don't mind, I might ride the bus to Birmingham for a few days to check on things, if you will be alright."

Austin frowned and said, "I guess I have been expecting it. We don't have kids for you to look after like some of the other wives, and you have a lot of responsibility as the owner of a business which they don't even comprehend. I will miss nights and morning coffee with you, but I do understand. When are you planning to leave?"

"No big rush I suppose. This is Friday. What if I leave Monday morning? The bus leaves at 0600. See, I am learning military time."

"I will get permission to go in at 7:30. I can not stand the thought of not seeing you off!"

"You big softie," Beth Ann smiled at him. She put her arms around him and squeezed. "We do have three days. We better make the best of it!"

Beth Ann left Lubbock around the first of February, but came back in Austin's car just in

252

time for her birthday on March 17th. The party was held on the base, and friends and other instructors and their wives attended. The base commander even put in an appearance and got to dance with the "Birthday Girl."

"Are we going to be able to keep Austin here, Commander, after he earns his wings? He wants to be fighting so bad."

"Beth Ann, I know how he feels, but he settled down a little after I had a talk with him. If Austin went to Europe right now, he would do well, no doubt in my mind, but what if he could train numerous pilots to be as good as he is? He and James can make a very significant contribution to the war doing just what they are doing. He takes his training of cadets very seriously, and he will be producing some of the best pilots around."

"Are we both being selfish wanting to not see him go?" she asked seriously.

"Probably some," he smiled, "but what he is doing is vital to our winning the war." He smiled at her as the song ended, and then he bowed a little bow and escorted her back to their table.

As Austin and Beth Ann got up to dance Austin smiled and asked, "Was he trying to get you to run away with him?"

"He asked, but I said no!" she squealed a small squeal as Austin squeezed her to him, and both laughed as people looked at them.

Chapter Twelve

June 1, 1944, Austin and James graduated from the flight training program at the Lubbock Army Air Base, and received their wings. The family had flown up from Little Rock and the base commander enjoyed showing Luke and Levi around the base while the officer's wives took off with the wives to eat some place fancy and encourage the wives with woman talk.

The next day they began their first training classes. The base commander spoke to the instructors old and new before he called a meeting of cadets and introduced each instructor.

"Men, within a week, the Allied Forces led by General Eisenhower will invade Europe in the largest assault in the history of warfare. There are several million troops involved. The cadets you will be responsible for training will be going up against veteran German pilots with excellent planes and nothing to lose. We are told to give them only 200 hours of combat training and send them. I understand the burden that will put on you and them, but we will do our best to see we send capable pilots to the front. God bless America!"

Each instructor was responsible for two trainees at first, but pilots were needed so badly the number jumped to four cadets each. Flying time was one and half hours a day for each of the cadets, which made for a long day sometimes for the instructors. Morale was not a problem, but fatigue sometimes could be.

The instructors stayed in shape as well as keeping their minds relaxed by grilling out steaks, hamburgers, chicken, and getting together as much as possible. However, sometimes on the weekends, Austin and Beth Ann, Payton and James would put the top down, and go for a drive through the surrounding countryside.

Lubbock, Texas, is built on a plateau and sits roughly at an altitude of 3202 feet above sea level. There are numerous small towns, lakes, and parks including Ransom Canyon, Roaring Springs, and Lake Sweetwater, which is only a three hour drive, and has been a spot for tourists and locals to swim and picnic since before 1900.

The foursome enjoyed their time off but Austin and James were wanting to be in Europe to help fight the war from the cockpit of a real fighter. It was the main topic of conversation.

It became apparent by October 1944 when the Allies captured the German town of Aachen the war was being lost in Europe. There was a seemingly endless stream of German troops from the front which had been surrounded and then surrendered. Hitler's general, Rommel, committed suicide after the fall of Greece. No one but Hitler believed the war could be won, and the Germans fell back to behind the Seigfrid line and began the Battle of The Bulge.

The Battle of the Bulge (also known as the Ardennes Offensive and the Von Runstedt Offensive) was a major last German offensive launched at the end of the war through the densely forested Ardennes Mountains region of Wallonia in Belgium, hence its French name (Bataille des Ardennes), and France and Luxembourg on the Western Front.

The Wehrnacht's code name for the offensive was Unternehmen Wacht am Rhine ("Operation Watch on the Rhine"), after the German Patriotic hymn Die Wacht am Rhein. This German offensive was officially named the Ardennes-Alsace campaign by the U.S. Army, but it is known to the English-speaking general public simply as the Battle of the

Bulge. The "bulge" being the initial incursion of the Germans put into the Allies line of advance, as seen in maps presented in contemporary newspapers.

The German offensive was supported by several subordinate operations known as Unternehem Bodenplatte, Greif, and Wahrung. Germany's goal was to split the British and American Allied line in half, capturing Antwerp, Belgium, and then proceed to encircle and destroy four Allied armies forcing the Western Allies to negotiate a peace treaty in the Axis' Powers' favor. Once accomplished, Hitler could return his attention and the bulk of his forces to the Soviet Armies in the East.

The offensive was planned with the utmost secrecy, minimizing radio traffic and moving troops and equipment under cover of darkness. Although ULTRA suggested a possible attack, and the Third U.S. Army's intelligence predicted a major German offensive, the Allies were still caught by surprise, due to a combination of Allied overconfidence, preoccupation with their own offensive plans and poor aerial reconnaissance.

Near-complete surprise against a weakly defended section of the Allied line was achieved during heavy overcast weather, which grounded the Allies' overwhelmingly superior Air Forces. Fierce resistance, particularly around the key town of Bastogne, and terrain favoring the defenders threw the German timetable behind schedule. Allied reinforcements, including General George

Patton's Third Army, and improving weather conditions which permitted air attacks on German forces and supply lines, sealed the failure of the offensive.

In the wake of the defeat, many experienced German units were left severely depleted of men and equipment as survivors retreated to the defenses of the Siegfried Line.

For the Americans, with about 500,000 to 840,000 men committed and some 70,000 to 89,000 casualties, including 19,000 killed. The Battle of the Bulge was the largest and bloodiest battle Americans fought in World War II.

The best part of hearing about the offensive battle to Austin and James was a significant number of the pilots trained by them were instrumental in destroying or neutralizing the Luftwaffe for the rest of the war.

Austin, however, had become even more reserved and unto himself. Beth Ann knew it was because he felt his time was being wasted. His one year commitment was up and he was to go before his base commander the next day.

"You want to go for a ride? I need to get out of Lubbock for a while. Pack a lunch and we will go to Ransom Canyon and eat."

Beth Ann put her arms around him and said quietly, "Austin, thank you for sticking this instructor thing out so that we could be together just you and me." She sighed a deep sigh and continued, "Have you thought about where you want to go? I want you to be fulfilled. I will go home to Alabama and keep myself busy until you come home."

"You are something else, Beth Ann. Your mother would be proud of you."

They spread a blanket on the rim of the canyon and she lay in his arms as they watched the last rays of the West Texas sunset turn the skies from blue to scarlet to indigo to darkness.

The next morning he knocked on the base commander's door after the attache had let him know he was there.

"Come in, Austin."

Austin stood at attention and the commander's face softened for he had grown to have a lot of affection for this young man, but he also knew that it was time to let him go. The war was over and he had done a job like no one else he ever had.

He said, "At ease. Have a seat," and he waved to a stuffed chair to one side of the room. The base commander sat down in an adjacent chair, and they both listened to an AT-6 leaving the runway and clawing for altitude. He turned to him after a moment and quietly asked, "Where do you want to go?"

The Supreme Headquarters Allied Expeditionary Force (SHAEF) under General Eisenhower issued a directive to create T-Force soon after the Normandy Landings. T-Forces were ordered to "identify, secure, guard, and exploit valuable and special information, including documents, equipment and persons of value to the Allied armies." T-Force units were attached to the three army groups on the western front; the 6th United States Army Group, 21st Army Group, and 12th Army Group. The targets of the T-Force were selected and recommended by the Combined Intelligence Objectives Subcommittee (CIOS). T-Force units were lightly armed but highly mobile.[1]

In post war Germany, T-Force was tasked with carrying out abductions of German scientists and businessmen. One of the objectives of these abductions was to recover Nazi military secrets. In addition to this, the abductions of the scientists enabled Britain and the United States to use their knowledge to build back up the British and American economy after the war, and also prevented the Soviet Union from obtaining their knowledge.

For example, Courtauld's received the latest information on manmade fibres, Dorman Long benefited from information and equipment originating from the Hermann Goering Steel Works, and even the British coal industry had pit props sent to them from the Harz Mountains. On the military side much information was gathered, which could have been vital had the war in the Far East not ended so soon.

Apart from this, there were wider political and economic implications, including the significance of the early liberation of Kiel, which prevented the Russians from adding Schleswig-Holstein and the Jutland Peninsula to their area of influence, as indeed they temporarily did with the Danish island of

Bornholm. The unit's role remained secret until very recently, coming to wider notice only with the publication of Sean Longden's book *T-Force, The Race For Nazi War Secrets, 1945* in September 2010.

Chapter Thirteen

The rough-riding Jeep with Austin and Hannah Olsen slowed to a crawl as they headed for the British sector of Berlin. Austin could feel the hair on the back of his neck tingle as if there were a cross hair zeroed in on it. He looked right and left and watched the mirrors for any sign of movement as they crept along.

Suddenly, a black Mercedes Sedan similar to what Hans Grubel had been driving pulled across the street in an area of close quarters where the rubble only allowed one car at a time, blocking it completely.

Austin stopped the Jeep and as the window in the back of the car began to lower, he hit the bright lights, grabbed Hannah by the hand and half dragged her out as they jumped from the Jeep.

"PLINK, PLINK, PLINK!" the sound of bullets from a gun with a silencer were hitting the Jeep as they ran for cover to the first darkened building. Austin did not know how many there were; so he just kept low and kept pulling Hannah till for a brief moment they stopped in an adjacent building after entering on the ground floor and racing up several flights of stairs. They waited and listened. He could hear German and Russian being spoken and after some curses in German the men returned to the car and sped away as another military Jeep turned the corner.

Barely allowing themselves to breathe even though they were gasping for air, they listened to two men going over the jeep, and talking in English among themselves quietly. In a few minutes, they could hear footsteps, and a voice said loudly but not yelling, "Captain Austin, is that you? Are you here?" It was the two MP's he had left at the pub!

As the men got closer, Austin said, "Don't shine your flashlights for they will know you found us. Is my Jeep okay?"

"Well, you got a few scars, but it is still drivable."

"Okay, go by it, turn off the lights and drive off. We will let you get about a block away, and then you turn at the first corner to the right and drive like Hades around the block and take up our rear! Got it? We will make a run for the checkpoint which is only a few more blocks, but I am depending on you two to keep them off us to let us get there!"

The two men were talking as if they had not found anything, stopped at the Jeep, turned off the lights, got in their's and took off at a good clip but nothing to cause anyone to notice.

Austin and Hannah made it to the Jeep, vaulted over the door entrance into their seats, and Austin started the engine but did not turn on the lights till they were moving. Just as soon as he turned on the lights, he heard squealing tires behind him pulling from an alley. He floored the Jeep, and turned to the left, ran between two still standing concrete columns, killed the lights and pulled his 45.

"May I pull my pistol, Captain?" Hannah whispered.

"Yes, but aim it somewhere out there!" He smiled.

The black sedan flew by in a cloud of dust, and Austin grinned to see the MP's Jeep not far behind with the passenger pointing a pistol and shouting for them to stop.

With the sedan not worrying about Austin for the moment, they drove quickly until the lights of the British checkpoint appeared out of the fog which was beginning to come down.

Seeing the British officer Hannah, the guard held up his hand in the curious, to an American, open handed British salute as he

273

passed her and Austin into the compound.

They pulled up in front of a well lit office building with several people coming and going, turned off the Jeep, and both took a deep breath. They got out of the Jeep, went up the few steps and into the outer office.

"Hey, Hannah!" cried one of the young enlisted men. "We heard some shots fired, did you happen to notice anything?"

Hannah smiled a little smile with a quick glance at Austin and said, "You know how it is. Could have been anything."

The briefcase was uncuffed from Austin's wrist by a British Colonel, who smiled at the two of them but did not open the briefcase. He took it toward an inner office and over his shoulder said, "You are free to go!"

274

Hannah walked out the door with Austin as he went back to his Jeep.

"I sleep here in the compound, and I suppose you are going back to the base."

"Actually, I have a room at a little hotel. As a member of T-Force, I get a few perks. In fact, I have a few days off. I will write a letter or two and see if I have any mail. I may even drive around in the daylight a little."

"Wow, you are living the high life!" she smiled.

"Meet me at the Berlin Pub tomorrow around 1100 hours, anywhere but the White Lily Pub! I will buy us lunch. The Berlin Pub is where most of the officers from T-Force hang out. No pressure, but I would like to get to know more about you."

"If you do, you might be disappointed. I am pretty much just a small city girl. But, I will be there."

The next day Austin was in uniform sitting with a group of other officers and he heard one of them comment on what had just walked through the door. He turned and looked too, and just for a moment, he did not recognize Hannah. She was in street clothes, and she was even more stunning than before.

Austin shrugged, "Oh, that's just my lunch date."

All the men were silent as he met her and walked over to another table. The conversation waned as people stared, but started again as Austin frowned at them.

"Behave!" he mouthed behind her back as

he escorted Hannah to their table.

Austin was enjoying the smiles and knowing winks and just shook his head.

"All men are dogs," he thought to himself.

Even he conceded she looked hot. She was dressed in a form fitting black and white patterned dress with black high heels. She had on a white hat that was broad brimmed and turned down on one side to not only make her look gorgeous, but it lent an air of mystery to her. Every male in the place was staring.

Austin helped her with her fur wrap, and she smiled and purred, "Thank you, Mr. Austin Johnson."

Austin could swear he heard one of the men groan under his breath. The air was charged with excitement. Austin realized

Hannah was used to just such reactions, but he still asked, "Had you rather go somewhere else?"

"Look, there is not a nicer place to eat in Berlin, and these guys are going to cry if we leave right now!" she giggled.

They both laughed as if it were an inside joke. She even went so far as to put her hand on his arm and lean over and whisper into his ear, "I know you are married, Austin, but we will give them something to talk about!" She laughed again showing her pretty teeth and smile. Every male in the place was wishing he was Austin.

Chapter Fourteen

With a few days of "down time" Austin drove around on the air base to look at the row of P-51 Mustangs. He got out and climbed up on one and looked into the open cockpit. He was dressed in uniform with his pilot's wings glistening.

"Hey, Captain Johnson, have you ever flown one of these?" It was Colonel "Big Red" Carmody from the base command.

He ran his hand over the cowl and said, "No, but I have always wanted to."

"Well, this is your lucky day. I can make it happen," said the man with enough gold braid on his hat to cause a solar flare. He was a full bird Colonel, and had been a squadron leader during the war. He confessed to Austin he was taking one up to just stay in practice, and he could fly wing man to help in case there were questions.

In a very few minutes, Austin had put on a helmet, jacket, and parachute and was climbing into the cockpit and getting a feel for what it must have been like.

He nearly shouted as the two planes lifted off the runway. He managed to maintain enough of a straight face to fly alongside Colonel Carmody who was enjoying the flight almost as much as he talked to Austin through the radio.

"I flew high cover for bombers during the

war as we bombed Berlin night and day. I never got tired of the feeling of diving through the clouds to engage the Germans in a dog fight. I have 12 confirmed kills of my own, plus a few more probables."

Austin smiled as he imagined what could have been. The two men chased one another through the clouds pretending to shoot at one another like kids with play guns tied to the handlebars of their bicycles as they pretended to be flying.

"Hey, Johnson, you are a heck of a pilot! I would have loved to be your real wing man!"

"Thanks, Colonel. It means a lot coming from you."

All too soon for Austin it was over. The men landed, put away the planes, and went to the ready room.

As they opened the door to the ready room, the base commander motioned for Austin to come to his office.

"We are not in trouble for joyriding in the Mustang, are we?" Austin whispered aside to Colonel Carmody.

"No way, look at the brass in that room. It is something much bigger than that!"

Even the Colonel snapped to attention and saluted.

"At ease, men. I want to introduce you, Austin, to your next assignment. This is Doctor Richard Weiss. He and Doctor Einstein and Werner Von Braun collaborated on several projects for Hitler, and he would like to go to America and work for our side. It may sound simple but we need you and Doctor Barnhardt to accompany him out of Berlin. His English is not as good as his German. Hannah can speak fluent German, and she will be helpful on your journey.

"Okay, how do we get him out of Berlin? I am sure the Russians and the rogue SS troops are looking for him too."

"You are so right, Austin. The three of you will be shot on sight if you are caught. We are smuggling him out tonight along with both of you. There is a C-47 loaded with farm tools ready to go from an old airfield beside the Rhine River. Can you fly it?"

"Sure."

"It will be dark in another hour. We can get you off the base, but after that you are on your

283

own!"

Austin took Hannah and the doctor to another room to change clothes. One of Hannah's scarves over the Doctor's long hair and one of her work dresses started the transformation. She put heavy wool white socks and farm shoes on him, and with an old tattered work jacket from a janitor they found he was ready.

Hannah told Austin to wait for a moment and then when she came out he could not believe it. She had on a male officer's uniform, and even a slight shadow mustache.

"Maybe I am going crazy, Hannah, but you <u>still</u> look sexy!"

"You're weird, Austin. We have papers, if we can wing it a little, as two soldiers escorting a sick widow back to Britain. Pray we don't have to use them. I doubt if we will fool many people."

"I agree, most male soldiers don't have breasts!"

"I don't have on a bra, and I have on a body wrap real tight."

"Let me see."

She slapped his hand away and said seriously, "This won't be a picnic if we are discovered."

"I am not taking it lightly. How am I going to explain to my wife if I get shot alongside you?"

"Maybe you better hope if you get shot they kill you, or your wife might!"

"That ain't funny!"

"It wasn't meant to be. Okay, we gotta go."

The guard at the gate had been alerted to let the threesome pass without stopping because the little old lady was very sick and the two soldiers were taking her home off the base."

The guard at the gate was one of the MP's which Austin knew, and he just saluted as the threesome eased through the gate. They were driving one of the base command cars which was a Mercedes Sedan. The windows were darkened and Austin was pleased with the power.

The war was over, and there were command cars coming and going all the time. Going down the city streets the car just looked like it was looking for a place to eat or a place to have a drink. No one seemed interested in the car at all.

Downtown Berlin had been bombed without mercy, but as soon as they cleared the city there were a surprising number of homes back in use. Austin drove fairly fast but did not want to draw any attention.

Soon, they saw the little industrial airport. The fuel trucks were pulling away as Austin came to a halt beside the runway.

"Hannah, I am going to walk across the runway and show the papers from the Colonel which state we are making a routine flight to southwestern Germany and Holland to deliver new farm equipment, and the little lady is very sick and needs to get to her home, which is just outside Amsterdam, our destination. As soon as you hear the engines start up bring Dr. Weiss carefully and load him. As soon as we get him on the plane, no matter what happens, we don't stop. Okay? Make sure the Doctor knows what the plan is. He seems to be pretty spry and he may can pull this off."

Austin drove the car to the steps and went up to the cockpit while Hannah, dressed as a male soldier, helped the doctor carefully up the steps. They had just shut the door and an orderly was driving the car away when another car came careening around the guard shack.

Austin had already started to roll and he had the engines revved all the way to the max. It did not take long for the C-47 to be moving fast enough the car could not keep up. A head and a luger were in one window.

"Get down and get behind something heavy duty. We are going to take some lead!" Austin shouted.

Just as the plane's wheels left the ground, the sound of gunfire erupted and there were bullets flying around inside the plane. Hannah had her body over the doctor and they were behind a stack of plow points on a pallet.

"Go! Go! Go, baby, go!" She could hear Austin yelling.

The load had been packed light on purpose, and as Austin pulled back on the wheel, the wheels took out a tree branch but they made it airborne!

As they circled for altitude, Austin was in constant communication with the base tower and finally received clearance to head southwestern for the English Channel and Amsterdam. His code name was "Plow Point."

He was flying without lights trying to make it to the empty countryside before anyone knew. He had been alerted already the Russians had two planes up looking for him. So, he could not fly at a high altitude and be seen on radar. He was flying very low and more afraid of hitting something than anything else.

All of sudden there were tracer bullets flying by the cockpit as a Russian Airacobra fired a warning salvo to try to force him to land. Since they had indeed found him, Austin reasoned, he might as well climb enough to be able to maneuver. The idea of being a ground level, slow moving, unarmed target did not sound like fun to Austin.

The C-47 with a light load climbed to about 10,000 feet without a problem. Finally, he could pick out the silhouette of the Russian fighter coming almost head on from a cloud bank. However, the Russian abruptly broke off and started a banking climb several hundred yards away, and he was almost perpendicular when a P-51 Mustang came roaring overhead with a burst from all 6 cannons, and in a second burst, the Russian plane exploded.

Suddenly, Austin's headset crackled, "Hey there, Plow Point! This is your flying buddy, Ol' Big Red, and I will be an overhead escort to the coast. Have a nice day!"

"Thank you, sir! You're the best!" Austin

exclaimed as he saw the fireball from the Russian plane drifting to earth .

The plane landed in Amsterdam, and British T-Force authorities came aboard and welcomed the group. They patted Doctor Weiss on the back and shook hands as Hannah translated to him he was safe now. The look of relief and joy brought tears to her eyes.

"I did not know Brits ever cried," teased Austin.

"I think I have something in my eye," she returned, a little embarrassed he caught her.

"Come on. I will buy you a drink."

"You're on! I think I just now let out the breath I have been holding!"

Chapter Fifteen

Hannah went to the airport to say goodbye to Austin and Doctor Weiss. They were flying back to Washington D.C. and Austin would ensure the doctor's safety as he traveled. From there he had a flight to take him to Birmingham. It was the second week of December in 1945, and he wanted to be home before Christmas.

"Do you know which plane you are taking home?"

"The base commander told me we were returning a B-24 back to the States. They are

293

not taking any chances with us."

"Austin, I gotta go, but you take care of yourself, okay? You are one of the good ones. As far as you and me; another place, another time." She smiled.

She didn't kiss him on the lips but she held him several long seconds before she kissed him on the cheek and walked away.

Austin picked up his duffel bag and took the good doctor by the arm, and as they walked toward the plane, he saw Hannah watching from a window. He saluted her and she blew him a kiss.

Once on the plane they had to wait a few minutes for the pilot and co-pilot. One of the men flying with them leaned over and in a joking tone said, "Believe it or not one of them is a female! She probably wants to take one last look at the map." He laughed, but it died on his lips as he looked over Austin's shoulder to see the female pilot glaring at him. She had a short, blonde, stylish haircut, piercing blue eyes, and a frown.

"I suppose you guys think you could do a better job?"

Austin turned around when he heard that voice and stood up. "Dang right I can!"

The pilot had her mouth open in surprise before she started laughing.

"Of all the men in the world which I know, you are the only one I would agree with! How are you doing, Cuz?" It was Anna Lee!

She grabbed him and hugged him tight. "Austin, no one from home has heard from you in months. James will be home soon. He was a fighter pilot in the Pacific flying the Hellcat. We did not know if you were alive or dead."

I am truly sorry for that, but T-Force is such a secret, security phobic place I was told to not contact even my wife until I got back to America. How is Beth Ann doing?"

"She has more Faith than any of us. She has never even considered the possibility you were not coming back.

I have a surprise waiting for you, Austin, when you get back to Washington. We land at 0600 their time, and I have been told a P-51 Mustang is waiting for you to continue on to Birmingham. You should be home about dark. It is a perk for being a hero! Some Colonel

Carmody put it together with a little help from General Talbert. Visit with you later!"

She hugged him, kissed him on the cheek as she teared up, and said tenderly, "Let's go home!"

The cab slowed to turn in to the Davis Estate drive, but Austin stopped him and said, "I want to surprise them."

The driver smiled as Austin handed him a 20.00 dollar bill and said smiling, "Merry Christmas!"

"Merry Christmas to you and yours, Sir!"

Austin picked up his bag, patted the man on the back, and said, "Thank you."

Beth Ann and the staff were finishing the evening meal in the dining room in the inner part of the house when the door bell rang.

"Who in the world?" said Beth Ann. "I am finished eating I will get it."

The big, double glassed doors were cut to see if someone was there but it was so distorted all Beth Ann could see was a uniform. Curious and concerned, she grabbed open the door quickly.

Samuel and the girls heard her scream. By the time they got to the foyer, Austin and Beth Ann were kissing and crying. Austin broke the kiss, and with Beth Ann's arms still around him, he reached and shook hands with Samuel and hugged the girls. They were all nearly hysterical with joy. The Prodigal was home!

THE END

Bibliography

1. Wikipedia Online

2. "A history of the world's airlines",
   R.E.G. Davies, Oxford U.P, 1964

3. Mintz, S. (2007). *Digital History*.
   Retrieved 11/2010 from
   http://www.digitalhistory.uh

Other books by
Don Horne:

Anthem To The Wind
Book 1/Beginnings

The story of twin sons of an itinerant Pentecostal preacher set in Arkansas in the early 1900's. From World War I adventures to business success in the movies and airline industry, history is entwined to make a captivating love story.

From Ann Margret
To Battle Stations

A coming of age/love story set in the 1960's and 1970's based on time spent aboard the carrier Kitty Hawk in Viet Nam. A story to be enjoyed over and over.